LUKE SUTTON:
INDIAN FIGHTER

LUKE SUTTON: INDIAN FIGHTER

LEO P. KELLEY

75150

DOUBLEDAY & COMPANY, INC.
GARDEN CITY, NEW YORK
1982

Library of Congress Cataloging in Publication Data

Kelley, Leo P.
Luke Sutton: Indian fighter.

I. Title.
PS3561.E388L835   813'.54
AACR2
ISBN: 0-385-17910-3
Library of Congress Catalog Card Number 81-43415

First Edition

LUKE SUTTON:
INDIAN FIGHTER

CHAPTER 1

Luke Sutton climbed the stairs that were attached to the side of the building that housed the ground-floor saloon. When he reached the landing on the second floor, he knocked on the door.

It was opened by an attractive woman with long blond hair and bright brown eyes.

"Luke!" she cried. "Oh, I'm so glad to see you. Come in."

"Nora, I came to tell you I'm leaving town."

She drew back sharply as if he had struck her. "Leaving," she repeated in a voice so low Sutton barely heard it. "I knew it would happen," she said softly. "Oh, I knew."

"That I'm a drifter."

"That I could never hope to hold you."

"Nora . . ."

"I knew from the minute I met you downstairs in the saloon. But I thought—I hoped . . ."

"Nora," he repeated, feeling helpless, not knowing what else to say. There *was* nothing else to say. He had known when he rode into this small town four days ago that he would ride out of it again and, in all likelihood, quickly. But, before he could do so, he had met her.

"Four days," she said. "Four wonderful days. I suppose I should be glad I had you for even that long. But after that first night we were together—the things you said, the way you—the way the two of us . . ."

"I truly wish I could stay."

"With a saloon girl?" she asked angrily, her eyes blazing.

"That's got nothing to do with why I'm . . ."

"All you did," she interrupted, "was use me, that's all! Just like all the other men who came before you." She lowered her head and her shoulders slumped. "Just like all the men who'll come after you."

How could he counter her charge? Sutton asked himself silently. He hadn't used her. He had shared something with her, something good, something that had been missing from his life for a long and lonely time. If he tried to tell her that, he knew his resolve might weaken. He wanted to stay with her. But he couldn't. He couldn't let himself stay. He didn't want to tell her why he couldn't stay. During the past two years he had told very few people why he must always move on, must keep searching, must remain a man alone.

"Why, Luke?" Her voice was plaintive and there was a stricken expression on her face.

He looked at her, unwilling to answer her question. He didn't want to talk about it. It was enough that he thought almost constantly about what he must do and why, his thoughts searing flames in an all-consuming fire.

"Luke," she said, "I tried. I tried to make you want me—no, I don't mean want me that way—not only that way. I know you don't love me. But I thought that maybe—it's only been four days that we've been together—and you've been so good, so tender to me. In time, I told myself, you might—well, like me enough to want to stay here with me. Or let me go with you wherever you feel you have to go.

"Where are you going, Luke? Why have you been asking all those questions of nearly everyone in town?"

"Maybe someday I can come back here, Nora."

She laughed and it was a hopeless sound. "I'm a drifter just like you are, Luke Sutton," she said. "In my business, you almost have to be one. When you come to a new place, oh, it's just fine and dandy at first. The men line up like hungry hands at a chuck wagon. But then, after a while, after the novelty wears off, the line's not quite so long any more. Then new girls come. So you move on and start all over again. We're two of a kind, Luke. Both of us are drifters. Each of us for our own reasons. I guess two of a kind's not much of a winning hand, is it? Anyway, if you came back here, I'd probably be gone and it isn't likely I'd have left word where I'd gone on the strength of a man's 'maybe.'"

There was nothing he dared say.

Nora said, "I shouldn't have gone with you that first night." She sounded as if she were talking to herself. "But there you were, standing so tall and slender and looking so strong, looking at me with those smoky gray eyes of yours, and when I came up and told you my name, you . . ." Her laughter rippled through the room. Recovering herself a moment later, she continued, "You *tipped your hat* to me! To *me!*"

"I've had me some good days and some bad days in my time, Nora," Sutton said very quietly. "These last four days here with you—they were some of the finest I've ever known and most likely ever will know, considering how things are with me."

She stepped toward him and rested her cheek against his chest. "Don't go, Luke! Not yet. Not so soon."

He gently kissed the top of her head and ran his strong fingers through her soft hair. "I have to move on, Nora. I've got myself no choice in the matter, sad to say. I should have ridden out long before this but you—we . . ."

She looked up into his eyes. "I think I love you, Luke."

Sutton closed his eyes and gritted his teeth. A muscle in his jaw twitched.

"Luke, did you hear me?"

He nodded.

"Doesn't what I just said matter to you? Not at all?"

"Nora, it matters a whole lot." He opened his eyes and nodded again. "It matters very much to me."

"But you're going to leave me."

He nodded a third time, finding it hard to meet her gaze.

She wiped away her tears that had begun to flow during the silence that had briefly surrounded them. "I'll put something up for you to take with you."

He waited on the landing until she returned and handed him a flour sack.

"I could make breakfast for you," she said, almost shyly.

He shook his head and then kissed her, holding her tightly against his body. Abruptly, he released her and went swiftly down the raw plank stairs that were attached to the side of the saloon, his sunburst spurs clinking on his black boots, and then made his way as swiftly to the nearby livery stable.

He loaded his gear onto his pack horse and then saddled and bridled his black. Minutes later, he left the livery, leading his pack horse.

He rode slowly up the main street of the small town, which, he had noticed when he rode into it, contained three saloons and one general store—but no barbershop or hotel.

He remembered thinking at the time that the town's establishments—and its lack of them—said a great deal about the nature of a man's life on the frontier.

He rode at a walk and promised himself he wouldn't look. He knew it would be better that way. But he did look when he reached the saloon and, as he had expected—hoped—he saw Nora standing at the top of the steps beside the open door that led to her room. When she saw him, she raised her arm to wave to him and then let it fall to her side without having done so. She took a tentative step forward as if she were about to descend the staircase to the street.

Sutton halted his horse. He touched the brim of his black slouch hat to her and then turned and rode on past the saloon, trying hard not to think about what was behind him, forcing himself to think of what lay ahead of him and of what he had to do.

He sat easy and tall in the saddle beneath the early morning sun as he rode along, sweat beginning to darken his blue flannel shirt and turn his face slick. He untied the black bandana he wore around his neck, used it to wipe his face, which was all sharp angles and rawboned planes, and thrust it into a pocket of his worn jeans.

Sutton's was a face that some might have called cruel, others merely hard-bitten or weather-worn. Thick black hair, ramrod straight, framed it, falling down his neck and over his ears. His body was notable mainly for its broad shoulders, slender waist, and lean muscularity.

He wore a cartridge belt strapped around his waist, its every loop loaded with a bullet for the Navy Colt which rested in the leather holster hanging from the belt. The revolver had ivory grips, a Mexican eagle carved in high relief inside a scalloped border on the left grip, and silver-plated straps and guard. Sutton had oiled the holster leather and filed the sight from his gun to insure a swift draw.

As the dirt street gave way, he rode out into grassland, the town—and Nora—behind him.

Grimly, he headed northwest, noticing as he did so that the grass was as dry as dust. No dew had settled on it during the night. Above him, the sky was a hazy blue, almost gray in places. The sun that illuminated it was still out of sight below the eastern horizon. The westerly wind blew steadily and Sutton noted that it overturned the leaves of several cottonwoods up ahead of him.

As he neared the trees, he rode through a blizzard of fluffy white seeds that were being torn from them and sent whirling through the dry air by the untiring wind.

The smell of sage, he noticed, was strong, sharper and more pungent than usual.

Storm coming, he thought. The signs were everywhere—in the dry grass, in the hazy sky, in the unusually strong smell of sage, and in the overturned cottonwood leaves.

An hour later, as he rode northwest into the Badlands, a mackerel sky loomed above him, the clouds drifting out in a long elliptical shape. High wind up there, he thought. Rain's riding it off to the east.

By midmorning the June sky had begun to darken and the hot air was no longer dry but faintly moist. Sutton spotted a creek in the distance and he knew it was one of the headwaters of the White River, toward which he was riding. He turned his horse to the left and spurred it into a trot. The pack horse's rope, which was wrapped around his fisted right hand, grew taut and he tightened his grip on it. He turned at the point where the creek began and followed it north. On his right was a slope covered with a thick mass of brilliant yellow wallflowers.

He rode on, not quite galloping, through a thick stand of Indian paintbrush and then around a gumbo slope whose multitudes of hummocks had been rounded and gullied by runoffs from the creek on his left.

An hour later a huge jagged barrier of eroded rock that was composed of cliffs, buttes, and ravines appeared on the northern horizon. As Sutton came closer to it, he was able to make out the desolation that lay between the tall line of rock and the northern bluff above the river. Rocks of every size lay strewn everywhere as if by the hands of careless giants. Among them grew isolated clumps of yucca. Gray-green sage clung tenaciously in places to the otherwise bare face of the looming rock barrier that jutted up from the ground and ran at right angles to Sutton's trail.

He turned his horse and headed west, following the curving creek that cut through the southern bluff above the White. He let his black pick its way down the bluff, which was over a hundred feet high in places.

When he reached the river's bank, he dismounted and flattened himself on the ground to drink. He spat out the mouthful of water he had taken in and wiped his lips. The water of the White, he had discovered, was filled with unsettled particles of clay. He decided the creek water was worth a try.

Back in the saddle, and with his pack horse trailing him, he rode back up the bluff and south along the creek until he spotted a small grove of elm trees off to the east.

Suddenly lightning flashed above the eastern horizon. Sutton looked up at the sky. It was no longer blue. Now it was an ominous gray.

Thunder muttered in the distance.

He got out of the saddle and, as his horses drank, he knelt between them on the creek's bank. Cupping the clear water in his hands, he used it to wash the White's silt from his mouth. Then he drank and, when he had had enough, he rose and led his horses to the distant grove of elm trees.

When he reached it, he took his ax from his pack and strode in among the elms. Twenty minutes later he had felled ten slender saplings from which he chopped the branches before hauling them out of the grove to a slightly elevated patch of ground he judged was a sufficiently safe distance from the grove, which might, he knew, be struck by lightning during the coming thunderstorm.

He got his rope that hung from his saddle horn and then bent down and pulled his bowie knife from his boot. After cutting lengths of rope with his knife, he crossed the ends of two of the saplings to form shear poles. He clove-hitched one end of the rope to one of the saplings, lashed it around the two trees, and tied another clove hitch. He spread the poles and firmly implanted their untied ends in the ground. Then he repeated the process with two other saplings, which he placed opposite the first two. He picked up another sapling and placed it in the notched ends of the four shear poles to form a ridgepole and lashed it in place with a half hitch.

Thunder muttered again as he implanted the ends of the remaining five saplings firmly in the ground, spacing them about a foot apart and slanting their other ends so that they leaned against the ridgepole. He lashed the end of each sapling to the ridgepole and then got his tarpaulin from his pack and laid it over the lean-to he had built, its open end facing east away from the westerly wind that was now savagely whipping the elms.

After placing stones on the tarpaulin to anchor it where it met the ground, he tied the cut end of his rope into a knot to prevent it from unraveling.

The thunder no longer muttered. It was now a loud rumbling. The sky was dark; the sun had vanished from it. Lightning blazed.

Sutton was stripping his horses when he felt the first drops of rain. The storm was going to be a big one, he told himself. The temperature had been dropping for the past hour. The air was now cool, almost cold.

He stowed his gear in the lean-to and picketed his horses in front of it. Then he bent down and entered it. Hurriedly, he untied his holster and then unstrapped his cartridge belt. He stripped the spurs from his boots, picked up his bowie knife, and proceeded to wrap it, spurs, Colt, and cartridge belt in his oilskin slicker. He left the lean-to carrying the bundle he had made and tied it to a low branch of an elm that was a safe distance from the lean-to.

Satisfied that he had rid himself and his immediate surroundings of anything that might draw a bolt of lightning, he returned to the lean-to, crouched, and entered it. He sat down and opened his saddlebag.

In the flour sack that Nora had given him he found goat cheese and slices of brown bread with honey between them. As he bit into the cheese, the storm broke.

Rain pounded down upon the tarpaulin over his head. The

wind tore at it with wild fingers. Jagged streaks of lightning split the dark sky and then thunder roared, booming through the river valley.

Hunched over far back in the lean-to, Sutton contentedly ate the bread and honey after finishing the last of the goat cheese. When the bread was also gone, he sat and waited for the storm to pass, thinking of his destination: the Black Hills in Dakota Territory.

In them he thought he might have a chance of finding one or both of the two men he was hunting. Gold, he knew well, had a way of luring all kinds of men, and Custer had found gold in the Hills two years ago—in 1874. Many of the men who headed for the Hills, Sutton also knew, were hard cases like the two men he was determined to track down. One or, if he was lucky, both of them might be there in the Hills. He intended to find out.

Outside the lean-to, the rain still flooded from the nearly black sky. Lightning still blazed and thunder still roamed noisily in the lightning's wake.

Sutton wrapped his arms around his bent knees, staring out into the wet gloom, thinking of everything that had happened to him during the past two years. Originally, he had hunted four men. He had found two. He was still hunting—and was determined to find—the other two.

Adam Foss was one, Johnny Loud Thunder the other.

He thought about them and about the other two while the rain pelted down upon the tarpaulin above his head. His thoughts scattered as lightning struck an elm in the grove and the blasted tree crashed to the ground with a sound that rivaled that of the thunder cannonading through the river valley.

Nearly three hours passed before the rain began to slacken. The water, which had formed a wet wall outside the entrance to the lean-to, finally became a shower and then stopped altogether.

When the sky began to lighten, Sutton left the lean-to and stretched to loosen his muscles, which were cramped from his recent confinement. The wind whipped raindrops from the leaves of the elms which made dark damp spots on his blue shirt.

He pulled up the picket pins so that his horses would be free to graze and, as they began to do so, he hunkered down and stared up at the sky that was rapidly clearing.

Once his horses had finished grazing, he intended to move on. He planned to follow the course of the White River as it snaked its way westward south of the great rocky barrier beyond its northern bank. Then he would head northwest again when he was past the rocky wall. He estimated that it would take him the better part of three days to reach the Black Hills.

He got up and returned to the lean-to where he gathered up his gear and carried it over to the pack horse, which was pawing at the wet ground as it grazed. He spent some time tying the gear on the animal, after which he put on the animal's bridle, from which trailed a length of rope.

His black, he noticed, had wandered down to the creek in the distance. He whistled to the horse, which merely raised its head, looked at him, and then ambled out into the water, dropping its head to drink.

"The dumbest dog's got more sense than that black," he said out loud, grinning to himself. He went back to the lean-to, picked up his saddle and bridle, took them to where the placid pack horse still stood, and dropped them there. He retrieved his folded slicker and the gear it contained from the elm branch to which he had tied it before the storm hit and carried it back to where his saddle and bridle lay in the wet grass. Then, after placing the still folded slicker beside his saddle, he started down toward the creek after the black.

He had taken no more than a few steps when he halted and, frowning, looked up at the sky. He had heard what he thought might have been thunder. Was there another storm hot on the heels of the one that had just passed? he wondered. He listened.

But the rumbling sound was too continuous and the sky was too blue for the sound to be thunder, he realized. Then— what?

When he felt the ground trembling beneath his boots, he swung around and looked south. A dust cloud hung in the damp air and, as he studied it, he was able to make out the humped forms of buffalo heading toward him. He glanced at the black standing in the middle of the creek. The horse, he decided, was probably safe where it was. But he knew he wasn't safe where he was because the buffalo were heading straight toward him. He turned and seized the rope that trailed from the pack horse's bridle, intending to lead the animal back toward the shelter the grove of elms afforded.

A loud whoop caused him to halt and look south again. Partially hidden by the shifting dust cloud raised by the stampeding buffalo were several mounted Sioux. Sutton saw one on the eastern side of the stampeding herd and two on the western side.

As he quickly jerked the rope in his hand, the pack horse

balked. He jerked the rope again and the horse dug in its front feet and threw its head up into the air.

Sutton swore and glanced south.

He was surprised to see how much ground the buffalo had covered since he last looked in their direction. And now, because they were so much closer to him, he could make out more Indians riding on both sides of the herd. They had formed two long lines, one on each side of the herd, both lines converging at a point immediately behind it. The V that the two angled lines of riders had formed prevented any buffalo from escaping from the bunched herd.

The Sioux whooped, the sounds they made much louder now as they shortened the distance between themselves and Sutton, who was considering abandoning his pack horse and making a run for the elms.

Why, he wondered, didn't the Indians use their rifles or lances on the buffalo? No lance had been thrown, no shot fired.

He jerked the lead rope and the pack horse swung his head to the left. The animal spotted the buffalo and its nostrils flared. It gave a mighty jerk and Sutton lost his grip on the lead rope. The pack horse bolted toward the trees.

Sutton raced after it.

But he never made it to the safety of the trees.

The Sioux who was riding in the lead on the eastern side of the herd spotted him, rode hard, and cut Sutton off from the grove. The Indian raised his lance and hurled it at Sutton, who jumped to one side. The lance landed, quivering, in the ground to his right. The Sioux raised his rifle, aiming at Sutton.

Dust filled the air as the westerly wind whipped it up from

the ground. The sound of the oncoming buffalo herd was deafening.

Before the Sioux could fire, Sutton was racing north ahead of the buffalo. He veered to the west, heading for the creek, planning to run along it and down into the river basin. Instead, he found himself running directly toward the Indian who was riding at the head of the western line of Indians that formed one spur of the V.

When the Indian saw Sutton coming, he grinned and prodded the buffalo closest to him with his lance, causing the animal to speed up its flight to avoid another painful prod.

Sutton realized that he couldn't make it to the creek. The Sioux ahead of him would see to that. But he knew he had to do something. In minutes—in seconds, if he didn't act fast— he would be crushed to death beneath the hoofs of the buffalo.

He began to run north as hard as he could. Although his heart was pounding and he could barely catch his breath, he kept up the pace he had set for himself, the noise the buffalo were making behind him goading him on.

He knew now what the Indians intended to do. He knew now why they had not shot at the buffalo and had not thrown their lances at them. They intended to drive them off the southern bluff of the river to their deaths on the jagged rocks that lined the river's bank far below the bluff.

Sutton, as he raced on, had difficulty maintaining his balance. His boots slipped and slid on the wet grass. But to fall now, he knew, meant a grisly death. He ran on, unsteadily but swiftly, toward the edge of the bluff that towered above the river.

He knew he had one chance—one slim chance—to avoid

being crushed to death beneath the hoofs of the stampeding buffalo. He also knew that to take that chance might mean an equally ugly death for him—his body pulped on the rocky riverbank.

He would have to take that chance. Certain death was the only alternative available to him.

He increased his speed, feeling as if his heart was about to burst. And then there it was—just ahead of him. The edge of the bluff.

Sutton raced toward it and, when he reached it, he leaped from it and went hurtling out into the empty air.

CHAPTER 2

For an instant Sutton seemed to hang suspended in the air. But then, arms akimbo, he was falling, twisting in the air, his hat torn from his head, his eyes seeing the river, then the bluff, the sky, the river again.

He hit the water hard and almost lost consciousness as he plummeted below its surface. Dimly, he wondered where the rocks that lined the river's banks—the ones he hadn't hit— were. And then, as he was whipped about in the raging torrent that the White had become as a result of the heavy rain that had fallen during the past several hours, he fought his way to the surface.

When he broke through it, he spit out the silty water he had swallowed and desperately sucked air into his lungs. His boots, filled with water, dragged him under and again he had to fight his way back to the surface, gasping for air, his lungs bursting.

It took him several minutes, during which he waged a constant struggle to stay afloat in the wild currents. When he was able to make out the broken and bloodied bodies of the buffalo at the base of the river's southern bluff, he began to swim toward the northern bank. It took him some time to reach it because of the dead weight of his waterlogged boots.

When he did finally reach it, he dragged himself out of the

river and lay among the rocks, breathing hard and still somewhat stunned as a result of having hit the water so hard.

He pushed himself up and, sitting among the rocks, looked
across the river at the dead buffalo. If he had not run so hard
—had not thrown himself with such driving force off the
bluff. . .

He blinked as water ran from his hair down his forehead
and into his eyes. When his vision cleared, he saw the Sioux.
They were rounding the bluff at the point where the creek
emptied into the river. When one of them pointed at Sutton's hat floating downriver, Sutton hauled himself to his feet
and quickly scanned the riverbank. He began to lope along it,
keeping close to the face of the bluff, which was in deep
shadow, in order not to be seen by the Sioux. He had not
gone far when he found what he had been searching for.

The river at flood stage in years past had eroded the base of
the bluff in places and Sutton, finding a deep cleft that had
resulted from the many years of such erosion, climbed up on
the natural shelf that had been formed and eased his body
under the rocky overhang.

From his dark recess he watched the Sioux on the other
side of the river. He could not hear them but he could see
that they were talking excitedly among themselves and scanning the surface of the river. Several of them were searching
among the broken bodies of the buffalo.

He smiled grimly. They wouldn't find him, not there, he
thought, not in that ugly litter of torn flesh and broken
bones. His smile vanished as he watched one of the Sioux
wade tentatively into the swiftly flowing river.

But then the man backed out of the river and returned to
his companions. Another Indian scouted along the riverbank

in both directions but then he too gave up the search for Sutton and joined the other Sioux, who were busily stripping the hides from the dead buffalo. Soon bright bloody carcasses lay exposed to the hot sun.

As the butchering proceeded, Sutton remained where he was, hardly moving, fighting the weariness that threatened to overwhelm him. He dared not, he knew, let himself sleep. When he found himself nodding, he scraped his hands along the ragged rock surface beneath him, drawing blood. The pain from his self-inflicted wounds kept him awake as the hours passed.

When the sun had slipped out of sight in the west, the Sioux began to load their buffalo meat on their ponies. It was a long process, too long to suit the impatient Sutton, who was eager to swim the river, get his horses and gear, and get out of the area before the Sioux returned, as he suspected they would, to gather up the remaining meat that they could not carry in a single trip.

Later, in the last of the sun's faint light, the Sioux, some running, some riding two on a single pony, made their way back to the creek and around the bluff.

When they had all disappeared, Sutton remained where he was, watching, listening. He saw and heard nothing. Still he waited.

The moon, almost full, was in the sky when he finally crawled out of his refuge, sat down on a rock, and pulled off his boots. He poured the water from them and then sat almost motionless, watching the southern bank of the river.

When he judged it safe to move, he stood up, stripped, tied knots in the ankle ends of his jeans, and then stuffed his boots, shirt, and longjohns into them. Carrying his bundle of

clothes in his left hand, he walked naked into the river.
When the water reached his chest, he began to swim, stroking with his free right hand while kicking hard with both
legs. He battled the strong currents and, when he finally
emerged on the southern bank of the river, he was far to the
east of where the buffalo slaughter had taken place.

He put his wet clothes and boots back on and then pulled
his bandana from the pocket of his jeans and tied it around
his neck. He began to make his way toward the creek, his wet
clothes cold against his body. When he reached the butch-
ered remains of the buffalo, he looked up at the top of the
bluff and then out over the river. He had never minded rain;
there was always some kind of shelter to be made or found,
but now he found himself thinking that he was more than
merely grateful for the rain that had fallen during the day
just ended. If that rain had not fallen to swell the river, he
knew he wouldn't have made it into the river despite the
great leap he had taken from the bluff. He looked down at
the piles of bloodied bones lying among the sharp rocks and
shivered.

He walked on until he came to the creek, which was sil-
vered by moonlight falling on its surface. He followed it
around the bluff and then upward. When he came out on the
top of the bluff, he headed toward the grove of elm trees. As
he approached them, he scanned the ground beneath his
boots, searching for his saddle and slicker. When he couldn't
find them, he began to fear that they might have been tram-
pled into dust by the stampeding buffalo. But, after checking
the tracks made by the buffalo, he was certain that he'd
dropped his saddle and rolled-up slicker between the buffalo
tracks and the trees. He back-trailed, thinking he must have

missed them in the not very strong moonlight. Then he walked in an ever widening circle. He found nothing.

He looked around him and found no sign of either his black or his pack horse. He made his way to the elms and searched among them but to no avail. The pack horse was gone. There was no sign of his black either.

And then he noticed that his tarpaulin was missing from the lean-to he had built earlier. The truth of the matter hit him then and hit him hard. The Sioux! They had taken his gear-laden pack horse. And his saddle horse. And his saddle and slicker in which he had wrapped his bowie knife, spurs, Colt, and cartridge belt. They had even taken his tarpaulin.

He thrust his hands into the back pockets of his wet jeans and stood motionless in the moonlight, staring at the uncovered lean-to. It was, he thought, going to be a long walk to the Black Hills. A helluva long and very dangerous walk, he told himself, unarmed as he now was and without a mount.

But before that walk began, he had the rest of the night to get through. He gathered up the leafy branches he had stripped from the saplings and spread them on the ground to form a rude bed. He lay down upon them, unmindful of his wet clothes, and was almost instantly asleep.

When he awoke, the sun was in the sky.

He got up and walked stiffly down to the creek, where he drank and splashed water on his face. The morning sun was hot on his back and his clothes were almost completely dry. The sun would soon dry them completely, he knew. It would also beat down on his hatless head as he continued his journey to the Black Hills on foot. He looked down at the torn-

up ground that had resulted from the passage of the stampeding buffalo and then at the grove of elms as if he expected to
see one or both of his horses standing under the trees. He saw
only his lean-to.

He was about to turn and follow the creek down the bluff
but then he hesitated. There was something about the lean-to
. . . Suddenly he let out a joyous yip and ran toward it.

Once beside it, he began to dismantle it, working fast, a
broad smile on his face. He had thought only minutes ago
that all he now had to his name were the clothes he stood up
in. But then, staring at the lean-to, he had suddenly realized
that he had more, much more, and what he had was of more
value to him here and now than dozens of double eagles
would be.

It took him two trips to haul all the saplings he had felled
down to the bank of the White.

Kneeling on the riverbank, he laid seven of the saplings
side by side and then lashed the trees together, weaving rope
under and over each one. Then he laid the remaining two
saplings at right angles on the seven to serve as crossbars. He
square-knotted them in place. After completing the task, he
tested all the lashings and was convinced that they would
hold.

He picked up the raft he had made and the single remaining sapling, which he intended to use to pole it, and carried
them down to the water's edge. He placed the raft on the
water and stepped onto it, holding the remaining sapling in
his right hand. At first the raft pitched and rolled beneath
him but he quickly gained his balance on it and poled away
from the riverbank.

The current was strong and by the time an hour had

passed the muscles in his arms had begun to ache. But he doggedly continued poling the raft past bleak bluffs that were pockmarked with swallow nests against which hordes of grackles launched their attacks in an attempt to seize the eggs and chicks of the swallows. For a time a meadowlark accompanied him, swooping above his head and then around the raft, warbling loudly, its yellow breast flashing in the bright sunlight.

The bluffs above the White's banks at times gave way to stretches of rolling grassland that were dotted with spruce. In places, eroded clay mounds rose like haystacks from the grasslands around which grew thickets of meadow rose and wild plum.

As the day wore on and Sutton, sweating heavily, continued poling his raft westward along the snaking course of the White, he began to think of food. He had been hungry for some time now, he admitted to himself, almost ravenous, in fact. He thought of his Colt. Of his bowie knife. He cursed the Sioux who had stolen them and the rest of his gear.

When the sun was almost down, he poled to the northern bank of the river, jumped from the raft, and then hauled it ashore. He was in the process of storing it safely for the night when he heard an ominous sound and recognized it at once for what it was. He stiffened and stood his ground, not moving a muscle. The rattling sounded a second time. Without moving his head, he examined the ground in front of him. Nothing. Slowly, he turned his head—and spotted the rattlesnake. It was off to his left and just behind him, its little eyes gleaming, the rattles on its upraised tail whirring, coiled to strike.

It was smaller than a diamondback, not quite three feet

long, he estimated. He knew it wasn't as poisonous as a diamondback but he also knew that its bite could make a man seriously ill.

There were stones littering the bank at his feet. Suddenly, in one swift and fluid motion, he leaped away from the rattler, turned, seized a stone, and hurled it at the snake, which had struck at him a moment after he moved. The stone missed the rattler's head but it tore a gaping hole in the snake's body. As the rattler writhed on the bank, Sutton picked up another stone, stepped forward, and slammed it down hard to crush the wounded reptile's skull. He kicked the dead rattler away from the raft and then went looking for a creek.

He walked over clay mounds and through meadows for some time but found no creek. He was about to turn back and settle for a drink of the White's silty water when he heard a resonant cooing and, a moment later, saw several male grouse emerge from a buffalo-berry thicket.

Sutton found himself salivating as he stared at the birds.

One of them suddenly spread its wings, lowered its head to ground level, and then dashed across the ground. Within seconds, its companions were whirling and bowing, strutting and stamping, all of them caught up in the frenzy of their mating dance.

Three female grouse, attracted by the males' dramatic display, ambled out of the buffalo-berry thicket.

Sutton automatically reached for his Colt and found only his hip. He swore softly.

He remembered hunting prairie chickens with a sling and stones when he was a boy. He'd been a fair shot then, he recalled, and he had put meat on his family's table more than once in those long-ago days. He briefly considered trying to down one of the birds with a thrown stone but then he rejected the idea. He'd only succeed, he believed, in driving them off because he didn't think he could throw hard enough to even injure his target. But a stone hurled from a sling, he knew from experience, had real power.

He swallowed the saliva that was flooding his mouth as, in the distance, a flashy male succeeded in mating with a female.

An image of the rattlesnake he had killed suddenly flashed through Sutton's mind. He began at once to race back to where he had left it and, when he got there, he picked up a stone and began to grind it as hard as he could against a larger stone. Once he had put a sharp enough edge on the first stone, he used it to skin the rattler.

He cut away two diamond-shaped sections of the tough skin and, after laying one on top of the other, he used his sharpened stone to punch holes in the two ends of the skin sections. Then he sliced thin lengths of snakeskin which he quickly braided.

He looped one end of the braided snakeskin through one of the holes he had made in the two diamond-shaped pieces of skin and knotted it tightly. He cut more lengths of snakeskin and repeated the process, knotting the second braid in the other hole in the diamond-shaped pieces of skin. He made a loop with a bowline knot in the end of one of the braids, picked up several round stones, and raced back to where he had encountered the grouse.

He arrived in the midst of a melee of mating. Good, he thought. They'll not be interested in me, seeing as how they have more important things on their minds. He placed a stone in the diamond-shaped pocket of the sling he had made, slipped the looped end of one braid over the middle finger of his right hand, and crooked it to hold the braid in place. He grasped the end of the other braid in his right hand and then, in a sweeping motion, he began to whirl the sling rapidly around his head, holding it out at arm's length. On the fourth whirl, as he straightened the middle finger of his right hand to release the looped end of the braid, the stone flew from the sling.

He scored a hit. But not a fatal one. The bird the stone had struck was flopping about on the ground, flapping its wings and trying to rise.

Sutton, dropping his sling, ran to it, scattering the other birds. He seized the struggling bird and deftly wrung its neck. He carried it back to where he had dropped his sling, which he picked up and pocketed. Then, whistling, the dead bird in his hand, he returned to where he had left his raft.

Sitting cross-legged on it, he plucked the grouse and then, using his sharpened stone, severed the head and legs from the body, after which he gutted it. He got up and scoured the area for wood and found, on the edge of a nearby expanse of grassland, a dead tamarisk from which he broke several branches. He carried them back to the raft and used one of them to spit the bird. He dug a hollow in the sandy bank and then broke one of the branches into small pieces which he placed in it. Over the branches he placed a layer of pin feathers that he had stripped from the grouse.

Taking his flint and steel from his pocket, he slid the D-shaped steel over the knuckles of his right hand and, holding the flint in his left, knelt beside the tinder he had prepared, and struck the flint with the steel. The first spark that sprang into bright life died before it could ignite the feathers. But the second, which was followed by a quick third, caught and Sutton, bending low, blew on the sparks. The feathers smoked and then began to burn. He continued to blow on the fire while feeding more feathers to the tiny flames.

The feathers blazed and then the wood beneath them caught and Sutton dropped back, his buttocks braced against his boot heels, watching with satisfaction as the fire continued to strengthen. He returned the flint and steel to his pocket, reached out, and picked up the spitted grouse. He proceeded to roast it, turning the spit slowly, salivating again as the bird's skin crackled in the fire and grease dripped from it to hiss and spit in the flickering flames.

When the bird was thoroughly roasted, he gripped both ends of the spit in his hands and began to devour it. He didn't mind the fact that, in his eagerness to appease his intense hunger, he managed to burn both his lips and tongue. Within minutes he had consumed most of the bird and then contented himself with tearing bones from it which he gnawed clean, one by one, until there was no more meat left.

The fire had burned low while he ate and Sutton contentedly watched it finally flicker and die out. He kicked dirt over its faint embers and then sat down, his back braced against a clay hummock.

In front of him the river murmured and around him the westerly wind blew, warm and rich with the fragrance of spruce trees through which it had passed on its eastward journey that, here in the Badlands, never seemed to end.

At times the wind dropped slightly and seemed to whisper in the deepening darkness. Sutton, listening to it, thought of Nora and the words she had whispered to him in their long nights together, of her soft touch, of her silken hair that was almost as bright as the sun, of the lively light in her eyes that danced the way the light of the pole star, which had appeared in the sky, was now dancing above him.

He experienced a sharp sense of loss that saddened him briefly until his thoughts ranged on and he thought of where he was going and why. The anger that had once been so hot and searing stirred within him as it always did at such times but now, two years after the night of its birth, it was hot no longer. Now it was cold and chilling. But just as deadly.

Sutton was still sitting on the bank, his knees up and his forearms crossed and resting on them, when the moon, as cold as the anger that was as much a part of him as were his hands or feet, began to climb the night sky.

Somewhere in the distance a wolf howled.

Sutton smiled when he heard the sound, feeling a kinship with the unseen wolf because, like it, he too was a hunter. He was a hunter of two men whom he intended to track down and destroy as ruthlessly as the wolf, roaming somewhere out there in the night it shared with him, would destroy its prey when it had at last run it to ground.

CHAPTER 3

The next day, when Sutton reached the point where the White flowed southwest, he poled to the north shore, abandoned his raft, and set out on foot in a northwesterly direction.

He walked until sundown, stopping only once to pick some dandelion leaves which he managed to chew and swallow despite their bitter taste. It was dusk when he came upon a stand of camas plants in full blue bloom. He dug up some of the plants, twisted off their slender green stems, and stored the bulbs in his pockets where the heat of the next day's sun would quickly dry them and make them fit to eat.

It took him two more days to reach the southernmost range of the Black Hills. Short grasses carpeted the gently sloping hills ahead of him, which were, in places, dotted with pine trees. Beyond them, a higher hill, which was completely covered with a dense forest of pine, undulated against the clear blue sky.

He halted abruptly when he heard the sharp sounds that he thought might be infantry picket fire. But then, when he heard the shouted string of curses ringing in the air, he knew for certain what it was that he'd been hearing. He began to lope around the fallen boulders through which he was passing, climbing up over them where they formed low ramparts, until he came out of the rocky landscape and was able to make out the line of pack mules in the distance.

There were twenty-two of them and, dancing irritably along the line they formed, his bullwhip snapping in the air, was an elderly mule skinner.

Sutton made his way toward the procession, angling in on it, as the sharp *pop, pop, pop* of the skinner's whip, which he had at first mistaken for gunfire, ripped through the air. As he came closer to the man and his mules, Sutton noted the break in the line. Some of the mules were moving forward in the front of the line but the remainder held back despite the skinner's efforts to move the balked and loudly braying mule in the middle of the line.

Eying the skinner's bullwhip, Sutton decided that it would be prudent to halt and hail the man before approaching him. The man might, he speculated, try to take out a stranger's eyes with that whip of his if he suddenly decided he had a need to defend himself. Or he just might put a hole in a stranger's heart with the Winchester he was carrying in his left hand.

The skinner, at the sound of Sutton's halloo, peered in his direction. Sutton moved forward slowly. He saw the skinner's eyes note the fact that he was wearing no gun and decided that he had indeed been prudent to call out to the man before attempting to join him.

"You lost?" the skinner asked when Sutton stood beside him.

Sutton shook his head and said, "I'm on my way to the Black Hills."

"On your way, are you?" The bearded skinner looked Sutton up and down and added, "You be *in* the Hills, mister."

"I know. I meant I was heading farther north," Sutton explained. "That the way you're going?" Sutton knew that it was but he felt the need to make conversation since the skinner, judging by his narrowed eyes and the way he was stroking his grizzled beard, was clearly suspicious of him and undoubtedly wondering about the reason for his sudden appearance on foot and unarmed in the hilly wilderness.

"I am," the skinner answered, "if'n I can move that blasted mule of mine what's holding up the parade." He hefted his twenty-foot whip, which had a hickory stock and was made of tightly braided rawhide with a knotted buckskin thong at its end.

"You mind if I take a look at that mule?" Sutton asked the skinner.

"What's there to see?"

"Looks to me like the animal's listing to this side some," Sutton commented, and then strode away from the skinner. When he reached the still braying mule, he got down on one knee and examined the animal's legs.

The rear left leg, he discovered, was the problem. He turned his head and beckoned to the skinner. When the man had joined him, he pointed to the leg and said, "Busted."

"Well I'll be damned!" exclaimed the skinner, bending over to stare at the broken leg. "Never did notice that. I must be slipping. I thought the critter was just being ornery as usual."

Sutton watched as the skinner examined the mule's leg.

"Got to shoot him," the man said ruefully, shaking his head. He dropped his whip and raised his rifle.

Sutton rose and stepped back.

The skinner's single shot echoed among the hills as the

downed mule thrashed violently, brayed weakly, and then died.

"I'll help you distribute its load among the other mules," Sutton said to the skinner.

The man shook his head vigorously. "They be loaded to their limit as it is and they've been toting their loads all the way from the steamboat dock on the Missouri. Looks like I'll just have to write off what that dead one was carrying."

Sutton stared at the load a moment and then said, "I could carry about most of that for you if you don't mind having me walk along with you."

The skinner stared at him in disbelief for a moment and then asked, "You fixing to run off with some of my goods should you get the chance?"

"Couldn't run very fast or far with most of that on my back." Sutton pointed at the load still tied to the dead mule. "Besides, you've got your rifle and I don't think I'd get far were I to try to run."

"My name's Bigby," the skinner said after a moment. "Virgil Bigby."

"Sutton. Where do you happen to be headed, Mr. Bigby?"

"Call me Virge. Dustville's my destination."

"Dustville's a mining camp?"

"You could call it that. Or you could call it a town. Started out, Dustville did, as a mining camp and grew itself into a right smart little town."

A town, Sutton thought. Where there's a town, there are men. Among them might be . . .

"It ain't one bit healthy," said Virge, interrupting Sutton's thoughts.

"What isn't?"

"Running around loose here in the Hills like you are without a gun of some kind or another. And hatless. You're asking for a case of heat stroke. Or maybe gun stroke, considering that the Sioux are also loose up here in the Hills." Virge cackled and spat a brown stream of tobacco juice that barely missed Sutton's boots.

"You're a hundred per cent right on that score, Virge," Sutton agreed amiably. "But I had myself a bit of trouble back yonder."

Virge asked what kind of trouble Sutton was referring to, his eyes suspicious again, and Sutton told him about his encounter with the Sioux hunters on the bluff above the White River.

Virge spat again when Sutton had finished his account of the incident. "This here's a real hard land," he observed laconically.

"You seem to be holding your own in it," Sutton commented. "You were moving those mules along at a pretty fast clip before that one you shot busted its leg."

"I been packing mules nigh on to thirty years."

"Some men prefer to use oxen."

Virge spat and then shook his head almost angrily. "Not me. Not by a long shot. Mules make better time than oxen do. They be a whole lot more sure-footed, too, which can be a mighty big blessing in terrain like this here. Course, you have your accidents from time to time." He looked down at his dead mule.

"But you have to pack grain to feed your animals," Sutton pointed out as he knelt on the ground and began to strip the load from the dead mule. "Cuts down on how much pay cargo you can carry, doesn't it?"

"It does that, there's no harm in admitting. But, son, I'm what you could call an entrepreneur. In business for myself is what I mean. I declare mules to be better'n oxen any old day and there's nobody can argue me down on that particular point."

As Sutton spread the dead mule's load out on the ground, Virge said, "Take the lighter goods—this here cloth, these sacks of beans. This rope. We'll leave the tools. Too heavy even for a back as strong as yours looks to be."

Sutton wrapped the items Virge pointed out in a tarpaulin and then hoisted the large bundle onto his back, allowing Virge to tie it in place on his shoulders.

"You're sure you don't want to back out on your offer?" Virge asked as he picked up his bullwhip.

"I'm ready to move out if you are," Sutton replied, shifting the load's weight until it rode comfortably, if heavily, on his back.

Virge cracked his whip, shouted a colorful obscenity at the mules, and they began to move forward once again.

The two men walked along in silence for a time, the only sound in the stillness that of Virge's whip popping.

"Damn it all to hell!" Virge roared as his whip struck the back of the lead mule from which blood and hair spurted up to dirty the surrounding air. "I try hard not to hit my critters. I've never in my life been one to abuse my animals."

Sutton, holding his hands under the pack riding on his back to brace it, said nothing.

After a time Virge said, "Fact is, I'm getting too damned old to be prowling around all over hell's half acre with only a bunch of stubborn mules to keep me company. When I was a young man—why, I could flick a fly off the ear of a mule and touch nary a hair on the critter's hide. But these here bulls is heavy sonsabitches to heft—this here one weighs near to six pounds—and nowadays when I snap it, I get a grabbing in my groin."

"There comes a time," Sutton said, "when a man wants to light in a place and settle down."

Virge blasphemed enthusiastically, whether at his mules or at Sutton, Sutton couldn't tell. "Where could a maverick like me settle?" he bellowed. "Got me no family, none closer than a cousin twice removed I ain't seen since Lincoln was a pup. Never did take myself time to marry." He grinned mischievously, revealing two gold teeth. "Never did need to." His grin widened. "I weren't half bad-looking in my prime and there were lots of girls, I can tell you, who noticed. But now—well, I don't belong to no particular place. So I keep packing. What else can I do?"

Sutton knew he was not really being asked to answer the question so he walked along in silence.

"Good place to stop up there," Virge said, pointing. "There's a stream. Fuel. It's open but the weather's fair."

When they reached the spot, Sutton dropped his pack and, without being asked, hunted for wood as Virge began to dig a fire pit.

"Creek's over thataway," Virge told him unnecessarily when Sutton returned and dumped the wood he had gathered beside the fire pit.

He took the coffeepot Virge handed him and filled it at the creek.

Twenty minutes later, as dusk settled, Virge fried bacon in a long-handled skillet, heated beans in a Dutch oven, and passed Sutton a slab of hardtack.

The two men ate in silence and, when they were finished, Sutton emptied his cup, relishing the last of Virge's strong black coffee. He picked up the plates, cups, skillet, and oven and carried them down to the creek, where he scoured them with sand and rinsed them in the water.

"Now then," Virge said when Sutton returned to the fire, "it's time for a treat. We'll have us a taste of Oh, Be Joyful." He got up and went over to one of his mules. When he returned, he handed a bottle to Sutton. "Strong stuff that," he said, "but powerful good. What's in that there bottle's no sod corn juice spiked with a little tobacco. That stuff in there's the genuine article!"

Sutton took the bottle and took a swallow of whiskey from it before passing it back to Virge.

Virge gestured impatiently. "Take yourself a man's drink, son! What you swallowed wasn't so much as a sip!"

Sutton's eyes were watering and his throat burning as a result of the fiery whiskey he had just drunk. Nevertheless, he put the bottle to his lips again, tilted his head, and took another drink.

"Now that there's the way to do it!" Virge exclaimed happily, apparently satisfied this time with Sutton's performance. He took the bottle Sutton held out to him and drained nearly half of its contents. "*Aahhh!*" he sighed, wiping his lips with the back of his hand. "Warms a man's body and delights his soul!"

Sutton put more wood on the fire as Virge pulled out his plug of Bull Durham and bit off a chunk. He chewed vigorously for a few minutes, his beard bobbing, and then fixed Sutton with a steady, black-eyed stare.

"You going to hunt about for gold here in the Hills?" he asked.

"Maybe I'll do some of that."

"Gold's here to be found." Virge looked down at the ground and then up at Sutton. "Here, have yourself another pull."

Sutton took the bottle from Virge and, under the old man's watchful eyes, drank more than he really wanted. He felt lightheaded afterward. He wondered how long it had been since he had last had a drink of whiskey. It had been, he remembered, that first night in the saloon with Nora. That night now seemed to him to be a world and a lifetime away.

"You wouldn't be looking for work by any chance, would you be, Sutton?"

"I work from time to time. Till I build up a stake. Then I usually move on."

"That's not any kind of answer."

Amused by Virge's sharpness, Sutton said, "I might look for a job of some sort once we hit Dustville. Might have to, seeing as how I haven't got a dollar to my name at the moment."

"Gambling?"

Sutton shook his head. "A woman, name of Nora."

Virge smiled knowingly. "Pretty, was she?"

Sutton, remembering, didn't answer immediately. And then, "She had long yellow hair and the most beautiful brown eyes I ever did see."

"I've always been partial to yellow-haired women myself," Virge commented. "She take you for all you had?"

"It wasn't like that. I bought her a dress. She didn't want

me to. I wanted to do it, so I did. But I didn't have much to start with and buying that dress cleaned me out."

"She looked good in it?"

"Prettier'n a painting."

"So how come you're here and she's—wherever she is?"

"Had me some riding to do."

Virge cackled and slapped his thigh. "But the Sioux set you down on your own two feet!"

"They did. They most surely did that."

"I could use a helper," Virge said abruptly.

"Me, you mean?"

"You're slender but you're strong. You got a clear, steady eye. Noticed your hands, I did—the calluses on 'em. I'd be willing to wager you could handle a bull almost as good as me—given a lot of practice, that is."

"I have a notion you could teach a man to flick a bull better'n most men could," Sutton said.

Virge ignored the compliment. He sat on the ground with his head lowered. "I never thought I'd hear myself say it, Sutton. Fact is, my two trips before this one—they was awful hard. So's this one turning out to be. I'm getting so I—I need somebody to lend me a hand. Oh, just now and then and from time to time, you understand." Virge lifted his head and glowered at Sutton. "I don't intend for anybody like you to try to take over my outfit, try to shove me aside and . . . So if you got any ideas of that stripe, you'd best just put them right on out of your head."

"Virge, I never yet have tried to take the place of a man I knew was better at what he did than I could ever expect to be."

Virge harumphed. And then he held out his hand to Sutton.

As the two men shook hands, both of them grinned.

After a breakfast of bacon and beans the following morning, Sutton volunteered to check the mules and their packs.

"Hold on!" Virge said. "It's time for some schooling."

Sutton took the coiled bullwhip Virge was holding out to him. He hefted it, nodded. "You were right, Virge. This bull's as heavy as some sidearms I've carried—even some carbines."

"Get yourself a good strong grip on its stock. But keep your wrist loose. Now do like this here." Virge demonstrated how to snap the whip, his hand fisted around an imaginary stock, his wrist twisting slickly as he flicked his imaginary whip.

Sutton imitated the gesture but failed to get the entire twenty-foot length of leather into the air.

"Put some more muscle into it," Virge advised him. "A whole lot more."

Sutton did and this time the whip cleared the ground in a somewhat limp S shape.

"You got to make that buckskin thong at the end pop," Virge told him. "Bring her up fast and high and then down just as smart as you can."

On his third try, Sutton was gratified to hear the sharp *pop* of the whip when he snapped it. He repeated the process. Another loud *pop*. The trick, he was discovering, lay not only in the way he gripped the whip's stock but also in the way he swung his arm.

Virge said, "You don't have to land that there bull on a mule to make him mind you. Just the sound of it whistling over his head or next to his ear'll usually do the trick. Specially if he's felt its sting once or twice in his life. Keep it up and over their heads. Make sure they see it in your hand. Of course, a little judicious swearing from time to time seems to help too."

Sutton offered the whip to Virge but Virge shook his head.

"You hang onto it. You can find out soon's we break camp whether you was cut out to be a mule skinner."

Later, the fire doused and the pack on Sutton's back once again, they were ready to leave their campsite.

But the mules didn't move.

Sutton picked up the whip and, judging his distance, aimed at a spot just above the lead mule. As the whip whined through the air and popped over the animal's rump, the mule brayed, flicked its long ears, and moved out. Sutton used the whip to send a message to the second mule in the line and it too moved out, hurrying up behind the leader. Sutton glanced at Virge.

"Not bad," Virge said. "Not the best but not bad."

Overhead, a hawk circled in slow sweeps across the cloudless sky.

"How far ahead's Dustville?" Sutton asked.

"Three, four miles the other side of that cliff dead ahead of us," Virge answered, pointing.

Sutton looked in the direction Virge had pointed and saw the massive cliff in the distance. The hawk, as Sutton watched it, swooped toward the cliff and alighted in a cleft on its side, flapping its wings as it settled down in its nest of broken branches.

"We got to get over that without wings?" he asked.

"We do. It be too far to go around. But there's a pass of sorts up in that cliff. I've used it before. These cliffs and hills, they've been hit hard by weather over the years. In winter, frost splits 'em. In summer, rain erodes 'em. The pass I mentioned, it cuts down pretty deep into that cliff. It's not as easy to get over as a dry wash would be. But it'll do for us. It'll have to unless we want to add a few more days to our trip, which I don't. See to the mules, Sutton, else they'll have you buffaloed in no time flat."

Sutton obediently cracked the whip, moving up and down the line of mules, the straps of the pack he was carrying on his back biting into his shoulders as he did so.

Virge led the way up the sloping side of the cliff, following a trail that was invisible to Sutton and which apparently twisted first one way and then another.

The mules pawed at the rocky surface and, their bodies slightly arched, pushed with their back feet as they made their way, one by one, up the cliff behind Virge.

Sutton, on Virge's instructions, had taken up a position at the rear of the line. He found that he could keep the mules moving easily enough simply by snapping the whip around the ears of the last two animals in line. They, to avoid being struck by the whip, nudged those in front of them and they, in turn, nudged the ones in front of them. As he followed them, loose gravel slid out from under his feet and once he almost lost his footing.

Virge, his hands cupped around his lips, shouted down to Sutton. "Through here!" He pointed behind him.

Sutton, looking up, saw the cleft in the cliff that had been formed, he guessed, by the erosion Virge had been talking about.

Virge moved on.

Then, so did the mules behind him.

Sutton, moving the mules along, soon entered the deep cleft in the cliff. He found himself walking along a narrow, nearly level ledge that wasn't much wider than the mule directly in front of him. Below him, on his right, the cliff's rocky side dropped down to form a deep ravine.

He could see Virge's head and shoulders above the lead mule ahead of him. He coiled the whip and, remembering Virge's earlier comment about the sure-footedness of mules, got a good grip on the tail of the last mule in line. It brayed a loud protest but Sutton hung on.

The procession moved slowly and, as it did, Sutton avoided looking down into the ravine on his right. He looked up when he felt pebbles strike his shoulders.

Above him on top of the cliff, a bighorn sheep was moving parallel to the pack mules. Its tawny body glowed in the sunlight and its curved horns arched gracefully over its neck.

Another damn fool, Sutton thought, that has to go climbing this staircase to the sky. He moved on slowly, holding tightly to the tail of the mule in front of him.

The bighorn began moving faster, heading in the same direction the pack mules were taking.

Sutton blinked, thinking for a moment that his vision had blurred. But no, now there were two bighorns visible on the edge of the cliff above him. As he watched them, a third appeared. All three suddenly began to run as if the sight of the men and mules below had startled them.

The biggest of the three, which was in the lead, passed above the spot where Virge was walking.

Sutton saw slivers of stone cascade down toward Virge as the rear right leg of the second bighorn slipped down over the side of the cliff that had been broken by the passage of the first animal.

Sutton let go of the mule's tail and shouted a warning to Virge as the second bighorn toppled off the cliff. The animal's body struck Virge and the lead mule, which was directly behind him. Virge lost his balance, flung his arms into the air, and, howling, fell off the ledge. Together with the lead mule and the bighorn, he went hurtling down toward the rocky floor of the ravine.

CHAPTER 4

Sutton dropped the whip, tore the pack from his back, and ripped it open. He seized the rope that was in it and immediately tied one end of it around an upward-jutting rock that was near the sheer wall of the cliff. Gripping the rope in both hands, he eased himself over the edge of the ledge. With both boots braced against the wall of the ravine, he began to pay out the rope slowly, working his way down into the ravine.

When he hit bottom, he let go of the rope and quickly scrambled over the boulders covering the floor of the ravine toward the spot where Virge lay moaning.

"Virge," he said when he reached the skinner, "I'm going to put you over my shoulder and haul you back up to the ledge. Now, it's going to hurt you some no doubt but . . ."

"First you haul a mule pack," Virge whispered, his breath wheezing between his bloodied lips. "Now you want to haul *me*. Sutton, you're more mule than man."

"I'll help you sit up, Virge."

As Sutton started to lift him, Virge let out a cry of pain.

"Told you it was likely to hurt some," Sutton said grimly.

"Let me be, Sutton. I'm finished—soon will be. I can feel it."

Sutton tried to lift Virge a second time but the skinner managed to push him away.

"Sutton, do you happen to be a God-fearing man like me?"

When Sutton didn't answer him, Virge said, "You'll say some sort of words over me, will you, when . . ." Blood gushed from his nose and he gasped for breath.

"Virge, I've got to get you up out of here—to Dustville where a doctor . . ."

"No doctor . . . Dustville."

"Virge . . ."

"In my pocket . . . paper . . ."

Not far away from where Sutton knelt beside Virge, the bighorn tried to lurch to its feet and fell back among the rocks. The mule lay motionless near it.

"Bill of lading," Virge whispered hoarsely. "Pocket . . ."

"Never mind about that now," Sutton said, reaching for Virge again.

"*Get it!*" Virge commanded.

Sutton searched through the skinner's pockets, found the bill of lading in one of them, and removed it. "I've got it, Virge."

"You know how to write?"

Sutton nodded.

"Pencil—in my pocket."

Sutton found it. Its point was broken.

"Write down what I tell you, son."

Sutton gnawed at the stub of pencil until he had made a new point.

"All my goods," Virge whispered. "My mules—I bequeath to . . ." He blinked once and said, "You never spoke your given name."

"Lucas."

"To Lucas Sutton."

"Virge . . ."

"You packed for me . . . didn't need to. Write down my words!"

Sutton wrote what Virge had dictated.

"I got to sign it," Virge said, trying to sit up.

With Sutton's help, he managed to do so. Sutton placed the bill of lading on a flat rock and held Virge steady as the skinner scribbled his name on the paper.

"Now lay me back down," Virge said and moaned. "Easy now."

Sutton cleared a space of rocks and then gently lowered the old man to the hard ground.

Virge's eyes closed.

Sutton remained motionless, kneeling beside him.

Minutes passed.

"Nora," Virge said, his voice barely audible. "Pretty, you said."

"I did, Virge."

"Go back to her. A man has to settle down sometime."

I can't, Sutton thought. "Virge, you got to let me try to get you to Dustville."

"Seen that town for the last time." Virge's right hand moved weakly. His eyes opened wide. "Sutton! Where . . ."

"I'm right here, Virge." Sutton took the skinner's groping hand in his own and gripped it firmly.

"Never did want to die all by my lonesome."

Several minutes later, the skinner did die. But not alone.

Sutton released his grip on Virge's hand, got up, and began to pile rocks on the man's battered and broken body.

When he had completed the task, he looked down at the

rocky mound he had made and said aloud, "I've done what little I could for old Virge, Lord. Now it's Your turn."

After pocketing the bill of lading, he made his way back to where the free end of rope dangled and climbed hand over hand back to the ledge. Once there, he untied the rope and remade and shouldered his pack. He picked up the whip he had dropped earlier and made his way carefully along the ledge until he reached the point where Virge had fallen. He bent down and picked up the skinner's Winchester, which lay on the ledge. When he caught up with the mules, which were gingerly picking their way down the sloping side of the pass, he followed them down, the whip coiled in his left hand, the Winchester clutched in his right.

Once all the mules were on level ground, he snapped the whip twice and moved them forward toward Dustville at a slow but steady pace.

As Sutton crested a hill an hour later, he caught his first glimpse of Dustville. The town lay nestled in a miniature valley formed by several surrounding hills which were sprinkled with low spruce and taller cedar trees. Ranging up from the town itself along the slopes of the hills on all sides was a profusion of log cabins, canvas tents, and a few simple structures built of unpainted wooden planks.

Dustville's single street, Sutton saw as he moved down the hill behind his mules, was bustling with life. Men crowded it. So did wagons of all kinds—flatbeds, modified Conestogas, and others that were little more than oversized carts.

All but one of the town's buildings consisted of single-story, false-fronted buildings. The exception was the two-story-high Gold Hotel.

As Sutton and his mules made their way along the crowded dirt street past signs that read Drug Store, Cabinet Maker, Livery, and Tin Shop, he pulled the bill of lading from his pocket and scrutinized Virge's cramped handwriting. Just above the addition he had made to it under Virge's urging was the name he was looking for: Bass and Farber. He gazed up the street and spotted a sign, crudely scrolled, that was nailed to a log building not far from where he stood. It said: Bass and Farber General Store.

When Sutton reached it, he herded his mules into the space between the store and its neighboring building and then, from a pile of logs that were stacked beneath an overhang covered with spruce boughs, he took several and managed to block both ends of the space between the buildings to keep the mules from straying.

He went into the store, carrying the whip and Winchester that had belonged to Virge, and asked a man lounging just inside the door where he might find the store's proprietor.

"That's one of them," the man answered, pointing the stem of his pipe at a man who sat in a slat-backed wooden chair that he had tilted back against the wall.

Sutton went up to the man and said, "I've got the goods you ordered from Virgil Bigby."

The man pushed away from the wall and the front legs of his chair slammed down against the board floor. He stood up, pushed his derby back on his head, and coolly appraised Sutton before asking, "Where?"

"The pack mules are corraled between your building and the one right next door." He handed the man the bill of lading.

The man looked at it and then at Sutton again. "Who

wrote this?" he inquired, tapping the paper with a dirty fingernail.

"I did. Virge told me to. Then he signed it, as you can see."

Several men, attracted by the conversation, joined Sutton and the store's proprietor.

"You're Lucas Sutton?" the proprietor asked.

Sutton nodded. "You're Bass—or Farber?"

"Farber. Where's Virge?"

"In a ravine up in that cliff south of town."

"What happened to him?" a brawny man blustered, scowling at Sutton.

Sutton told him what had happened, noting that the man wore no gun.

Farber frowned and said to the man who had angrily questioned Sutton, "Poor Virge. Well, it's his bad luck."

"And Sutton's *good* luck," the man responded. He took a slender nail from a keg beside him and began to pick his teeth with it. "Virge getting killed is good luck for Mr. Sutton here."

"Now, Denton," Farber said. "Hold on a minute."

Sutton kept his eyes on Farber, who was studying him with a skeptical expression on his face. "We had to leave some tools and things behind," he told Farber. "One of the mules broke a leg. Virge shot him." He wriggled free of the pack on his back and lowered it to the floor. "You'll find some of the goods the mule was carrying in there."

"Fell off the cliff, you say?" inquired a short man with a potbelly bulging between his suspenders, which were draped over a soiled white shirt.

"That's what I said," Sutton told the man.

"How many times you reckon has Virge brought in supplies to Dustville, Denton?" the paunchy man asked.

"Three by my count," Denton replied. "And he ain't never fell off any cliff before either. Course he was always traveling alone before."

"It happened the way I said it happened," Sutton declared, his voice low as he turned to face the man named Denton.

"Maybe it did," Denton said. "And maybe it didn't."

"Can you prove it didn't?"

"Can you prove it did?" Denton tossed the nail he had been using as a toothpick back into the keg. "I'm thinking maybe you pushed Virge off the cliff after you got him to sign his goods over to you. Or maybe you shot him off the cliff with that Winchester you're holding."

Farber asked, "How many cartridges you got in that thing, Sutton?"

"You're welcome to check," Sutton said, holding the rifle out to Farber.

Denton intercepted it, checked it, and said, "One shot fired."

"The mule with the broken leg, remember?" Sutton said, his voice steady as he reached out and pulled the Winchester from Denton's hands.

"That broken-legged mule fits real convenient into your tall tale, Sutton," Denton said. "This whole business don't smell so wholesome to me. What you got to say about it, Farber?"

"Well, it might have happened the way Sutton says it did," Farber answered hesitantly.

"I am not a quarrelsome man, Mr. Farber, Mr. Denton," Sutton said quietly. "But if a quarrel comes calling on me, I'm only too happy to jump right in and take my part in it."

The man with the potbelly caught the glint in Sutton's eyes and backed away hastily. He eased behind Denton and then hurried toward the door.

From the corner of his eye Sutton saw two other men quickly leave the store.

"I think you killed Virge," Denton said bluntly to Sutton. "To turn yourself into a rich man almost overnight."

Sutton brought the rifle in his hand up to hip level, his finger tight on its trigger. "I won't shoot you, Denton. Not if you do what I say. That goes for you too, Mr. Farber."

"Yes, sir," Farber spluttered, eying the rifle. "Yes, sir, Mr. Sutton."

"Now then, Mr. Farber," Sutton said, his rifle aimed at the top button on Denton's broadcloth trousers. "If you'll be good enough to saddle two horses and bring them around to the front of the store, I'll be much obliged to you."

"Right away, Mr. Sutton." Farber scurried out of the store.

When he had gone, Denton said, "Now wait up, Sutton. I was just talking. I didn't mean for you to take what I said so serious."

"But I did take it serious, Denton. I took it real serious."

"I was just talking!" Denton whined, his hands reaching out in front of him as if to ward off the barrel of Sutton's Winchester.

"That's the point, Denton. You were just talking. And you will, like as not, go right on talking. Only thing is, I want to make sure you got all the facts to talk about. If you don't have them, why, there's just no telling when a liquored-up lynching party won't decide to set out after my hide for the murder of old Virge, thanks to you and all your talking."

"They're here, Mr. Sutton," Farber called from the doorway of the store. "Right out front. The two horses you wanted."

Sutton bent down and opened the pack he had been carrying. He removed the rope he had used earlier, turned to Denton, and said, "Move, Denton. You and me are going to do some riding."

"Wait a minute, I . . ."

Denton moved when the barrel of Sutton's Winchester jammed into his chest. Sutton followed him out the door and, as Denton climbed into the saddle of one of the horses Farber had supplied, Sutton handed his whip to the store's proprietor. "We'll be back directly after Denton's had a chance to do a little sight-seeing up in that pass I told you all about. I want him to pretend he's a Pinkerton man. I want him to convince himself that I didn't kill Virge Bigby. If he doesn't do that, well, he's one loose talker, Denton is, and who knows how many men might take it into their heads to listen to his foolishness and wind up stalking me for a crime I didn't commit?"

"You're not going to kill him, are you?" Farber asked in evident alarm.

Sutton's eyes widened in mock surprise. "Gracious me, no! I'd never shoot an unarmed man. Besides, I've got no reason to kill him. At least, not so far, I don't."

When Sutton was aboard the other horse with the coiled rope hanging from his saddle horn, he said to Farber, "While you're waiting for me and Denton to get back, I suggest you check the merchandise I brought you against Virge's bill of lading and have my money ready for me. I'll be wanting it real bad."

"Yes, sir, Mr. Sutton," Farber said, his head bobbing. "I'll be sure to do just that. How long will it be before you return?"

"Depends, Mr. Farber, on how good a cliff climber Denton here turns out to be."

Denton blanched.

Sutton looked around at the faces of the men who had gathered in front of the store and who were watching him as he sat his horse, his rifle angled toward Denton. "Denton and me wouldn't object to some company on this little expedition of ours, now would we, Denton?"

Denton opened his mouth to speak but no words came from it.

"What I mean to say is," Sutton continued, "there seems to be a question of whether or not I murdered old Virge. You gentlemen could consider it your civic duty to ride along with Denton and me and find out what's true and what's false." His rifle swung around and pointed at a thin man with a sallow complexion.

The man looked at the rifle that was aimed at him. His lips tightened into a thin pink line and he slowly nodded.

"Fine," Sutton said as the man unhitched a horse from the rail in front of the store and got into its saddle.

"You?" he asked another man with a checkered shirt, his rifle swinging around to point in the man's direction.

"I'll go," the man said quickly. "Glad to."

"Then let's ride," Sutton said. "You three go first. I'll bring up the rear."

No one spoke as they rode. When they reached the base of the cliff, Sutton called a halt.

All three men turned around to look at him.

"Denton," he said, "you and me are going to climb up that slope to the top of the bluff on the right there." He gestured and Denton got out of the saddle and started up the slope. Sutton dismounted and did the same.

Ahead of him, Denton crawled upward, occasionally dislodging stones which rumbled down around Sutton.

When they reached the top of the bluff, Sutton said, "Up ahead there is where that bighorn went over the side. You go on over there and take yourself a look around."

"What am I supposed to be looking for?" Denton asked nervously.

"Tracks. *My* tracks. Maybe you think I came up here and chased—or shot—that sheep I mentioned off the bluff."

Denton moved forward.

Sutton watched him go.

A few minutes later, he returned.

"What'd you see?" Sutton asked him.

"Nothing."

"You didn't see the tracks of any bighorns?"

"I saw *them*. I mean I didn't see anything else."

"How many were there?"

"Three."

"Just like I said."

"Just like you said. Sutton, listen, I don't want to . . ."

"We're going back down now, Denton." Sutton waved Denton around him with the barrel of his Winchester and then followed him down to level ground where he told Denton to tell the other two men what he had—and hadn't—seen on the bluff, which Denton obediently and eagerly did, glancing, as he spoke, from his listeners to Sutton and back again.

"Now we're going on foot up through the pass," Sutton announced, removing the coiled rope from his saddle horn. "You two first," he said to the two men who had remained silent during Denton's recital. "Then you, Denton. I'll be right behind you."

They left their horses, reins trailing, at the base of the cliff and climbed up into the pass. When they reached the place where Virge had fallen, Sutton tied one end of the rope he had brought with him around an upward-jutting rock.

"Come here, Denton," he said. When the man stepped up to him, he put down his rifle and tied the free end of the rope tightly around Denton's waist.

"Wait!" Denton cried, trying to undo the knots Sutton had tied. "I'm not . . ."

"Yes, you are," Sutton said flatly, picking up his rifle again. "You're going down there and you're going to take those rocks off Virge and you're going to try to find a bullet hole in his body of the kind made by a shell fired from a Winchester."

"Wait a moment, Mr. Sutton," said the man in the checkered shirt.

"What for?" Sutton snapped.

"There's no real need to make Denton go down there. We can see the mule and the bighorn lying down there."

"And the broken ledge up above there," said the other man, pointing upward.

"So we know it happened like you said it did. The sheep

fell and hit Virge and the mule—we can see it happened just like you said it did."

"Can you now?" Sutton said. "But you can't see Virge. Maybe I did shoot him like Denton said I did. Denton, let's go. Over the side."

While Sutton and the other two men watched in silence, Denton eased himself over the ledge, paying out the rope as Sutton had done earlier but with far less skill. He was only a few yards down when he began to swing in a circle, bumping against the rough side of the ravine.

"Use your feet!" Sutton shouted down at him. "Brace them against the wall of the ravine!"

Denton tried to do so but his efforts were less than successful. He bumped his way down until he was almost at the bottom of the ravine. Just before he reached it, he lost his grip on the rope and it slid through his clenched hands. He let out a yell and then another one as he hit the bottom of the ravine. He lay there a moment and then he struggled to his feet and made his way over to the ominous mound of rocks.

From the ledge above him, Sutton and the other two men watched him as he proceeded to uncover Virge's body.

Five minutes later he yelled up to them. "Help haul me up! I can't make it up on my own."

Sutton hauled him up.

When Denton stood once more on the ledge, Sutton stared at him, waiting for him to speak.

"Virge didn't have no bullet holes in him," Denton said in a faint voice. He dropped his gaze and stared at the palms of his hands, which were raw as a result of the rope burns he had suffered during his descent.

"Your pants are ripped," Sutton observed, "and there's some blood in your hair from your fall but you're in one piece. If you have a notion to talk once we get back to Dustville, I reckon you'll have something to talk about now." He turned to face the other two men. "You two satisfied with my story now?"

They both nodded.

"Then we might as well head back to town," Sutton declared.

Once there, Sutton found Farber standing behind the counter of his store. "I left those two horses you were kind enough to loan me hitched out front," Sutton told him.

"Fine, Mr. Sutton. Now about your account. I've got everything all toted up here. I'm sure you'll find everything in apple-pie order."

Sutton set his rifle on the counter, accepted the sheet of paper Farber handed him, and studied the figures written on it. "You made a mistake, Mr. Farber." He handed the paper back to the storekeeper.

"A mistake, Mr. Sutton?"

"That sum should be *six* hundred and eighty-one dollars. Not five hundred and eighty-one."

Farber frowned and then, uneasily, said, "Why, you're perfectly correct, Mr. Sutton. I did make a mistake, didn't I?"

Sutton held out his hand.

Farber bent over, twirled the dials of a safe that stood behind the counter, opened it, removed a cash box, and, after placing it on the counter, counted out the money and put it in Sutton's outstretched hand.

"Much obliged," Sutton said. "You can keep that bull I

gave you before I left here. I don't expect I'll be needing it now. You can also keep the mules—or sell them."

A man wearing a faded flannel shirt, dusty trousers, and boots with one heel missing entered the store and came up to the counter.

Sutton stepped away from it and began to count his money.

"What can I do for you?" Farber asked the man at the counter.

"Well," said the man hesitantly, "if you really want to do something for me, you can grubstake me. I'm a little down on my luck at the moment—I've been panning up in Twisted Creek and I *know* I'll find color if I can just hold out a little bit longer."

Farber was frowning at the man with apparent distaste. He said, "I'm not in the grubstaking business. I run a general store—on a cash-and-carry basis only."

"Please, mister," the man pleaded, "I only need maybe twenty dollars—fifteen'd do—to buy me some food. I got all my tools, a tent, and my rocker and . . ."

"Try the second house up on the north hill," Farber said. "Mr. Linden's been known to grubstake fellows like yourself from time to time."

Sutton looked up quickly from the money in his hand.

"Thank you," the man at the counter said to Farber. "Second house on the north hill, you said? I certainly do thank you mightily for the recommendation." He turned and practically ran from the store.

Sutton stepped up to the counter. "Did you say 'Mr. Linden' just now?"

"I did."

"Would you happen to be referring by any chance to Mr. Samuel Linden?"

"Why, yes, I was. Do you know Sam?"

Sutton thrust the role of bills into his pocket and picked up his rifle. "Me and Sam used to do business together down in Texas. I wouldn't mind meeting Sam again. It's always nice to talk over old times with a good friend."

"Second house on the north hill," Farber said. "That's where you're likely to find Sam."

Sutton nodded and left the store. He started walking north along the dusty street when a sign that read: Good Food Served Within caught his eye. He realized that he was hungry and went into the building from which hung the painted sign that had caught his eye. He found himself in a room that was cluttered with wooden tables and chairs. In a corner several men occupied one table, among them the man in the checkered shirt who had accompanied Sutton and Denton earlier. They looked up from their food as he entered and began to speak in low tones among themselves.

Sutton sat down and placed his rifle on the table. A moment later a young man came out from behind a cloth-covered doorway in the rear of the restaurant and asked him what he'd have.

He ordered two steaks, corn-meal mush, fried potatoes, pie, and coffee.

While he waited for his food to be served, he avoided glancing at the men in the corner. He suspected they were talking about him—him and Denton. It wouldn't be long, he thought, before everyone in town knew what had happened up on the cliff. That, he decided, was just fine with him.

When his food was set before him, he cut a piece of steak

and began to chew it. Not beef, he thought. Buffalo. The taste of the meat reminded him of his brief employment as a buffalo hunter in the Nations. That was the first time he had tasted buffalo meat.

He lingered over his coffee when he had finished his meal and, when the young man who had served him appeared with a coffeepot in his hand, Sutton nodded, and the man filled his cup a second time. When his cup was empty again, Sutton picked up his rifle, paid his bill, and went outside.

As he was climbing the hill north of town, he saw the man who had been seeking a grubstake in Farber's store coming down the hill toward him. The man, smiling broadly, greeted Sutton.

Sutton acknowledged the greeting with a nod and asked, "That Mr. Linden's place up there?"

"That's it. Right up there. Mr. Linden, now he is one fine man, let me tell you. If you're looking for a grubstake, you could do worse than talk to Mr. Linden. He just loaned me forty dollars."

"Hope you find some gold," Sutton said.

"Oh, I will!" the man said, breaking into a broad smile. "I've got every confidence I'll find some color before too much time passes me by. Sweat and stick-to-it's my motto."

"Best of luck to you," Sutton said, and continued up the hill. When he reached Linden's house, he knocked on the door.

It was opened almost immediately by a neatly dressed middle-aged man.

Sutton said, "Hello, Sam."

Linden studied Sutton's face for a split second and then he beamed and threw his arms wide. "Luke Sutton! Well, won't

I be damned!" He threw his arms around Sutton and hugged him, taking Sutton's breath away momentarily. Then he released him and stepped back. "Luke, it's good to see you, it truly is. Come in, come in!"

Sutton followed Linden into the house.

"Sit yourself down, Luke. Make yourself comfortable. Lean your rifle against the wall." Linden sat down across from Sutton on a horsehair sofa and crossed his legs. He took a long nine from a humidor and struck a match. After puffing furiously for several seconds, he dropped the match, took the cigar from his mouth, and roared, "So you finally decided to come looking for gold, Luke!"

"How've you been, Sam?"

"Fit as a fiddle. My hair's starting to go gray on me but there's lots of life still left in this old boy. But what about you, Luke? What've you been doing since—how long's it been since we saw each other last?"

"Two years, Sam. We were having a drink together in the Alhambra back home in Texas. It was the day before you were going to head up here. You'd just sold your ranch."

"I remember now." Linden puffed on his cigar. Ash fell to the floor unnoticed as he stared across the room at Sutton. "Those broncs you used to bust and sell to me—they were the best of the best, Luke. I take it you're not busting broncs for a living any more?"

Sutton shook his head.

"Well, tell me what you've been doing with yourself."

"Some of this, a little of that, Sam. I've been on the move a lot during the past two years."

Linden studied Sutton. "You weren't exactly a homebody back in Texas but then neither were you fiddle-footed, as I recall. You and Dan used to . . . Is he with you, Luke? Is your brother here in Dustville too?"

Sutton shook his head again. "Dan's dead, Sam."

Linden's jaw dropped and for a moment, obviously stunned by what Sutton had just told him, he didn't speak. Then he asked, "What happened to him, Luke?"

"He was murdered," Sutton replied. He proceeded to tell the story of what had happened to him and Dan that night in Texas two years earlier. A feeling of relief swept over him as he talked frankly and openly for the first time about what had happened.

"The bastards!" Linden exclaimed angrily when Sutton had finished his story.

"I caught up with two of them," Sutton said. "One last year—down on the Mexican border. Another one I settled with in Dodge City the year before that. Neither one'll do any more murdering."

"And you're still after the other two. That's why you've been on the move. That's why you're here. Am I right?"

"You're right, Sam. Their names are Adam Foss and Johnny Loud Thunder. Johnny's a breed." Sutton described both men. "You happen to have seen anybody around who might be them?"

"No. I can't say I have."

Sutton leaned back in his chair, spreading his legs out in front of him and clasping his hands over his waist.

"That Sheriff Britton," Linden mused, "he's not the smartest lawman in the West. Imagine him accusing you of murdering your brother!"

"Well, it kind of looked like I might have done it, Sam. The jury went and decided I did. There's a five-hundred-dollar bounty waiting for the man who brings me in dead or alive."

"I hope nobody tries to collect it."

"One man did last year. Try, I mean." Sutton grinned.

"Do you plan on staying here in Dustville for a while, Luke?"

"I might."

"If you don't find this Foss or Johnny fellow here, though . . ."

"I'll be moving on."

"I liked Dan," Linden said thoughtfully. "He was a real good boy. Clean cut. I remember how he used to like to read books. He read books the way a drunk downs whiskey. Which reminds me. I'm remiss in my manners. I've got some fine bourbon. I'll get it."

Sutton waved a hand. "Not for me. At least, not right now. Sam, did you find gold? Did you strike it rich up here?"

"I gave up hunting for gold before my first year up here was over. I guess I'm a businessman at heart. So I went into business."

"You were always a good businessman, Sam. You started that ranch of yours on a shoestring and in three years you had the biggest and most profitable spread in central Texas."

"Nice of you to say so."

"It's the truth."

"Now I'm part owner—a silent partner, you might say—in several businesses in town. The livery, the general store, the hotel—I run a logging camp not far from here. But, best of all, I'm in the grubstaking business and I do get a kick out of it though it's a gamble. But then so's life. I got into it in an accidental sort of way. A young man I knew—his name was Leeds—was down on his luck. This was right after I got to

the Hills. A good man and bad luck—that's always a bad
combination. I loaned him twenty dollars and, by God, Leeds
parlayed that twenty dollars—found gold, he did—into seven-
teen thousand dollars in two *months!* He had promised me
fifty per cent of any gold he found and he paid off, good as
his word. It's happened to me several times since the same
way.

"Grubstaking's like a game—a challenge. I try to pick win-
ners. Mostly, I do. There was a young down-at-the-heels
fellow here just before you came. I've seen him around town
—and not in the saloon down in the hotel neither. I lent him
forty dollars just now. There's no telling what I'll wind up
with. Maybe nothing. But I think I can tell good men from
bad."

"Well, Sam, it's getting dark out. I'd best be heading back
to town—to the hotel."

"Damned if you will! You're staying right here. I've got a
spare room. You hungry? I pay a man to come in and cook
my meals for me. He'll be here soon."

"I've eaten, Sam, and . . ."

"How long has it been since you slept in a bed, Luke?"

"It has been awhile, Sam."

"I've got a bed with a real mattress on it in the spare room
and that mattress isn't stuffed with just straw or rushes either.
And the pillow—it's full of the softest goose down you ever
laid your head on. Now, what do you say, Luke?"

"I say you've always been a good friend to me, Sam. Even
now—now that you know I might mean trouble for you since
I'm a wanted man."

"You'll stay here in my home then?" Linden asked
brusquely.

"I will, Sam. Be real glad to, to tell the truth."

CHAPTER 5

When Sutton awoke late the next morning, he yawned and stretched in the soft bed before swinging his legs over its side and sitting up.

He could hear Linden moving about in the other part of the house beyond the closed door of the bedroom. As he dressed, he thought of the money in the pocket of his jeans. And then, with a feeling of sorrow, of Virge Bigby. He thought of Linden and his friend's concern for him, which had been expressed in the way he had insisted that Sutton was welcome to take a bath in his galvanized tub before going to bed. Sutton ran his fingers along his smooth cheeks. Linden had lent him a straight razor after he had bathed, and the stubble that had covered his cheeks and chin was now gone. He felt like a new man, clean, rested, and ready for whatever the world might have to offer him—good, bad, or indifferent.

He pulled on his boots and opened the door of the spare room.

"Morning, Luke!" Linden called out cheerfully from where he sat in an upholstered chair near the window. He took off his glasses and put them, together with the newspaper he had been reading, down on the small table that stood next to his chair.

"Nice day, looks like," Sutton said, glancing through the window.

"Luke, I can't cook worth a tinker's damn," Linden said, "but I've got a pot of coffee on the stove. Want a cup?"

"I could use one."

"My man will be here before long. He'll cook you something to eat."

"I could do for myself if that's all right with you, Sam."

"It's fine with me," Linden said as he got up and poured a cup of coffee for Sutton. "There's bread, butter, and eggs in the larder over there. Delivered fresh only this morning by Bill Lamoreaux over on Eagan's Flat. He keeps me well supplied. Help yourself."

Sutton drank from his cup and then went over to the larder in which he found the food Linden had mentioned. As he took a frying pan down from the wall, he asked, "You eat yet, Sam?"

"Just had some coffee. Never was much of a breakfast man."

"From the look of where the sun's at, I'd say it's more near to dinnertime."

"Well, I could eat an egg or two, I suppose."

Sutton set about making their dinner. He fried eggs and then, after setting the table that stood near the stove, pronged one of the stove lids aside and, sticking a fork in a slice of bread, toasted it over the flames of the wood fire.

Later, as the two men were finishing the meal that Sutton had prepared, Linden jabbed a knife in the direction of the table by the window. "I read a headline in that newspaper over there this morning that says Custer's heading west from Fort Lincoln."

"Another gold-prospecting expedition?"

"Not this time. The headline said Custer's got Indians on his mind. He plans to wipe them all off the face of the plains, I gather."

"He may be just the man to do it."

"He may be," Linden agreed. "But it's a damn shame the way the Indians haven't got a chance in this country even though most of them don't know it or won't admit it. It's only a matter of time before they'll be wiped out completely, and those that aren't'll end up on reservations. I don't know which one of those two fates is the worse one."

"Well, while a man's got a breath left in him, he's also got a hold on hope, no matter how loose that hold might be."

"There's no such thing as hope on the reservations," Linden boomed, a trace of bitterness in his tone. "It's plain tomfoolery, it is, asking people who've been nomads to settle down in one place and paw about in the earth, pretending to be farmers on land that won't grow anything worth the notice of even a locust. The agents give them putrid meat after they've sold off the good stuff to settlers, which just happens to be illegal. And making all those rules and regulations—enough to fill a mile-high stack of ledgers—for those people to live by. Who the hell do we think we are anyway, acting like God's own anointed sent to make true believers out of the Indians, who just happen to have their own set of truths that have stood them in pretty good stead for a long time before we whites ever came crowding into their country?"

"The Sioux haven't taken kindly to us tearing up the Black Hills," Sutton said. "They say this is their sacred ground."

Linden's face went slack and his anger seemed to dissipate.

"Truth to tell, Luke, I feel guilty as sin even just being here like I am. I feel like a thief."

"From the point of view of the Sioux, Sam, that's what you—and me and all the rest of us here in the Hills—are."

"But the gold . . ."

"The gold," Sutton repeated as Linden's voice trailed off. "Yep, there's the matter of the gold, now isn't there?"

Before Linden could comment, there was a knock on the door. He rose from the table and opened the door. "Good morning, Brock!" he said. "Come on in. I think there's some coffee left in the pot. I'll pour you a cup."

The man who came into the room was tall and broad-shouldered and, Sutton thought, he seemed uncomfortable inside a house.

"Ira Brock," Linden said, "meet Luke Sutton. Luke's a friend of mine from the old days down in Texas."

Sutton rose and shook hands with Brock.

"Brock oversees my logging operation," Linden told Sutton as he handed Brock a cup of steaming coffee and sat down again at the table. "Best logger that ever came down the pike, Brock is, Luke."

"I heard mention of your name in the saloon last night, Sutton," Brock said, seating himself at the table.

"You did?" Sutton met Brock's appraising gaze.

"Your name and Denton's," Brock added.

Linden glanced from Brock to Sutton, a question in his eyes.

"Denton and me," Sutton said to him, "we had ourselves a bit of a set-to yesterday when I first hit town."

"That's what I heard spoken about," Brock said. "Seems Denton didn't take too kindly to what you made him do."

"I'm not much surprised to hear that," Sutton remarked. "But it needed doing, which you can understand if you got the whole story and got it straight."

"I did and I can't fault you, Sutton."

"What's this all about, Luke?" Linden asked.

Sutton told him. He concluded by saying, "So Denton's learned now that it's not wise to sling mud on a man's name —at least not on this man's name."

Linden frowned. "Denton's a ne'er-do-well. Hangs out with some hard cases who drift here and there in the Hills. I'd steer clear of him if I were you, Luke."

Brock cleared his throat and, when Linden glanced in his direction, said, "Mr. Linden, I came over here to talk about what we're to do about that stand of timber on the north end of Eagan's Flat."

"Sam," Sutton said, "I think I'll mosey on down into town and have a look around."

Linden's eyes met Sutton's. "You do that, Luke, if you've a mind to. But . . ."

"Yes, Sam?"

"Be careful, Luke. And I'm not just talking about Denton, if you take my meaning."

"I do, Sam, and I will. Be careful, I mean. Nice to have met you, Brock." Sutton strode to the door and went outside.

The sun, which was riding high in the sky, struck his head like a hot fist as he walked down the hill toward Dustville, which lay sprawled below him.

When he reached the town, he went into the general store and found Farber behind the counter, busily weighing beans for a customer.

He walked over to some plank shelving on one side of the

store and stood, hands thrust into the back pockets of his jeans, staring at the hats that were piled one on top of the other on one of the shelves. He tried on a slouch hat, found it too big, tried another that was too small. His eye was caught by a black Stetson, flat-topped and flat-brimmed. He put it on. It was snug but it felt right. He went over to the window and stared at his reflection in the glass.

"Very dapper, I must say," Farber said from behind Sutton, rubbing his hands together. "Suits you, Mr. Sutton, if I may say so. Yes, it most decidedly does."

Sutton adjusted the Stetson, cocking it at a slight angle, and then turned around to face Farber. "I need a six-shooter. Cartridges. A gun belt and holster."

"Right over here, Mr. Sutton. If you'll just follow me, please." Farber led Sutton to a glass case, which he unlocked with a key he took from his pocket. "I've Smith and Wessons and, of course, Colts of several kinds. Do you have a preference in sidearms, Mr. Sutton?"

Sutton's gaze ranged over the revolvers in the case.

"Now here," Farber said, "is a fine example of the Colt .45. Note the pearl grips." He placed the gun on top of the case. "Quite rightly called the Peacemaker." He chuckled.

"Let me have a look at that Russian-model Smith and Wesson," Sutton said, pointing to the gun.

"Most of my customers prefer Colts," Farber said. "They . . ."

Sutton held out his hand to Farber.

Farber took the single-action .44 from the case and placed it in Sutton's hand.

Sutton tested its balance, his second finger resting lightly on the steel spur below the trigger guard. He let his thumb come to rest lightly on the small hump above the gun's walnut grips. "You mentioned that your customers, most of them, preferred Colts," he commented, and twirled the Smith and Wesson. "Bill Cody prefers this gun. Maybe on account of its cartridges have a whole lot more lead in them and a little less powder than the American model. You got cartridges for this?"

Farber turned and rummaged about on his heavily laden shelves. "Ah, here we are!" He handed a box of cartridges to Sutton.

"I'll take two boxes." When Farber had handed him a second box, Sutton said, "Now I'll need a good knife. A cartridge belt. A holster."

Farber spread his wares on the counter and Sutton chose a sheathed hunting knife and a black leather cartridge belt.

"This holster," Farber said, pointing to one lying on the counter, "is very nicely hand tooled and it . . ."

"Don't want one with a flap. Haven't you got any without a flap?"

Farber sadly shook his head. "The nearest thing I have to what you want is this one here."

Sutton took the holster Farber handed him, unsheathed the knife he had just bought, and cut off the thin leather strap that was designed to go over the trigger guard and button in place on the holster's face. "Now it'll do just fine."

"You want to be sure of a fast draw, I see," Farber said, stepping back from the counter slightly.

"I do," Sutton said soberly as he filled the belt's loops with cartridges. He strapped it around his hips, holstered the Smith and Wesson after loading it, and shoved the knife into his right boot. "Now then, how much do I owe you in all?"

Farber told him and Sutton paid for his purchases. As he accepted his change, he asked, "Did you ever happen to hear by any chance of a man who calls himself Adam Foss?"

"Adam Foss?" Farber thought for a moment and then shook his head. "I don't recall having heard that name before."

"How about a breed named Johnny Loud Thunder?"

"I'm sorry, Mr. Sutton."

Sutton turned and left the store. Once outside, he headed for the saloon that occupied the right wing of the hotel and, once through its batwings, he went up to the bar and ordered whiskey. When it came, he left it untouched in front of him. He made small talk with the bartender for a few minutes and then said he was looking for two men. He named and described Foss and Johnny but the bartender claimed never to have seen or heard of them.

As Sutton headed for the batwings, the bartender called out to him.

"You didn't finish your drink!"

"Didn't so much as start it," Sutton called back. "Help yourself to it."

Outside, he lounged against the wall of the hotel, his eyes darting from face to face as men passed in the street or rode by on wagons. Minutes later, he straightened and made his way into the shabby lobby of the hotel, where he went up to the desk and spoke to the room clerk.

"I'd like to have a look at your register."

"Why?" the clerk asked belligerently.

"Let's just say I have a consuming curiosity about the names of the men who had the real strong nerve to rent a room in a run-down place like this." His right hand, apparently accidentally, slapped against the butt of his holstered .44.

The clerk caught the gesture, looked into Sutton's stony eyes, and hastily shoved the register toward him.

As the clerk ducked into a back room, Sutton turned the thick book around and began to leaf through it, running his index finger down the list of names.

Adam Foss's name did not appear in the register. Neither did that of Johnny Loud Thunder. Of course, Sutton told himself, they could be using other names by now. But checking the register had been worth a try. He turned and made his way out of the hotel lobby into the bright sunshine spilling down into the dusty street.

He walked up the street and began to climb the hill toward Linden's house in the distance. He halted when he heard a man call his name. He turned around as the man came up to him.

"I heard all about you and Denton," the man said, smiling. "Now that was some sort of show, I hear. Wish I'd been around to see it."

Sutton was about to continue on his way when the man asked, "Where you from, Sutton?"

"No particular place."

"You here to grub for gold?"

"You do have a thirst for knowledge, don't you?"

"Just wanted to make the acquaintance of a man like yourself. Just wanted to see what kind of man it was could turn Denton into ten times a fool."

"Well, now you've seen him. I'll be on my way." Before he could turn, a fist caught Sutton from behind, landing in the small of his back. Almost at the same instant, he felt his .44

pulled from its holster. He spun around to find a big man standing only steps away from him, his Smith and Wesson stuck into the man's waistband.

The man slammed a fist into Sutton's face, sending him reeling backward toward the man who had been speaking to him. That man seized Sutton's arms in a tight grip and yelled, "Give it to him, Kent!"

Kent landed a right in Sutton's mid-section and followed it up with a hard fast left. "How's that, Darby?"

Sutton doubled over, the breath *whoooshing* from his lungs. He gasped for air and, as he straightened up, he heard a new voice behind him—a voice he recognized as belonging to Denton.

"We got him!" Denton shouted gleefully. "Oh, we sure got him now!"

"*You* don't, Denton," Sutton snapped, struggling to break the grip of Darby, who was still pinioning his arms behind him. "Your two hired hands have. Don't you have the sand to do your own fighting?"

Denton stepped around in front of Sutton, his teeth bared in a feral grin, his hands clenched at his sides. "You've set a lot of people to talking about me, Sutton," he snarled. "And I don't like what they're saying." Denton drew his arm back and then rammed a small fist against Sutton's jaw. "Not one little bit, I don't like it!"

The brassy taste of blood filled Sutton's mouth. Then, as Denton prepared to land a second blow, he dug his heels into the ground and pushed backward. His action unbalanced Darby, who was still behind him and still gripping his arms. Both of them went down. Sutton rolled to one side, got his feet under him, and came up fast. His right fist sank into Kent's stomach and, as the man doubled over, grasping his mid-section, Sutton landed a right uppercut on Kent's jaw. Kent went flying backward, stumbling and then falling hard.

Sutton raised his right forearm to ward off a blow Denton was aiming at him. Then he reached out, grabbed Denton by the shirt collar with one hand and by the waistband with the other. Sutton sent him careening into the trunk of a locust tree.

As Denton screamed in pain from the impact, Darby jumped Sutton from behind. Sutton bent over and threw Darby over his head.

Kent was on his feet and coming toward Sutton, blood flowing from his lower lip, which Sutton had split open.

Sutton bent down, picked up the groggy Darby, raised the man high above his head, and then threw him directly at Kent.

Kent hit the ground, Darby a dead weight sprawled on top of him.

Sutton waited a moment and then, when neither man made a move, he strode over to where Denton was struggling on his hands and knees, trying to rise. He hauled Denton to his feet, turned him around, and said, "Too bad there aren't any witnesses to this little shindig. If there were . . ."

Denton brought his knee up and savagely slammed it into Sutton's groin.

Sutton, pain dizzying him, lost his grip on Denton. He bent over, clutching his groin, the locust tree in front of him suddenly blurring before his dazed eyes.

Denton gave him a kick that caught him at the base of the

throat and he let out a strangled groan. As he did so, he seized Denton's ankle before the man could get his foot back on the ground, twisted it hard, and threw Denton to the ground.

As the pain raged in Sutton's throat and groin, he bent over and hauled Denton to his feet again. He was about to smash his fist into the man's face when Kent suddenly seized him by the shoulders and pulled him backward.

Sutton released Denton, spun around, and his fist that had been about to smash into Denton's face smashed instead into Kent's. Kent careened backward, gagging. He spat a cracked tooth from his mouth.

Sutton returned his attention to Denton, who lay on the ground, propped up on his right elbow, holding up his open left hand toward Sutton.

"Don't!" he cried, his hand trembling.

But Sutton did. He picked Denton up, rammed his back up against the locust, and then, holding him by the throat with his right hand, hit him hard in the chest with his fisted left. He drew back his fist and then sent it flying again, this time to crack against Denton's quivering jaw.

Denton's head slumped forward.

When Sutton released him, Denton slumped unconscious at Sutton's feet. Sutton looked over his shoulder. Darby and Kent were also on the ground. Kent wasn't moving. Darby was crawling away through the grass.

"Hold up!" Sutton yelled at him.

Darby froze.

Sutton strode over to him and, looking down at him, said, "You've been keeping awful bad company, Darby. A man like Denton over there's bound to bring you trouble in one shape or another. This time it was me. Next time—you take my meaning, Darby?"

Darby nodded nervously as he remained on his hands and knees in front of Sutton.

Sutton said, "Should any of you take a notion to come looking for me again, you'll find me up at Mr. Sam Linden's. I wouldn't want you to have too much trouble finding me."

"I don't want to ever—ever in my life—set eyes on you again, Sutton," Darby muttered.

"Now that seems a shame, since we were only just starting to get acquainted."

"Let me go," Darby pleaded. "Can I go?"

"I got no kind of hold on you."

As Darby got shakily to his feet and began to stagger down the hill, Sutton went over to where Kent was lying. He bent down and pulled his Smith and Wesson from Kent's waistband, glanced at the still unconscious Denton, and then holstered his .44 before making his way up the hill, the pain in his throat and groin like two low-burning but very hot fires. As he walked, he spat several times, a blend of saliva and blood.

He found Linden's house empty. For a few minutes he wandered aimlessly through it and then he pulled the chair by the window around, sat down in it, and propped his boots on the window sill. He stared out at the rolling hills and the trees that swayed gently in the westerly wind. The sun streamed in the window, so he pulled his Stetson low on his forehead to shield his eyes from the bright glare. He crossed his ankles and shifted in his chair.

The pain in his throat and groin gradually lessened as he sat by the window considering his next move. Should he stay with Linden a while longer? Pay another visit or two to Dustville, ask his questions of a few more people, keep scanning the street for those two unforgettable faces? Or should he move on?

Irritated with his own indecisiveness, he started to get up from the chair, to search for something—anything—to do. His gaze fell on the newspaper lying on the table next to the chair. He picked it up, unfolded it, and snapped it to straighten it out.

He scanned the news of gold strikes and then turned the page. The major story on the next page was about Custer. Sutton recalled Linden having mentioned noticing its headline earlier.

As he read the article, he learned that Custer and the Seventh Cavalry were about to head west from Fort Abraham Lincoln. The Seventh's destination, according to the article, was the spot where Rosebud Creek ran into the Yellowstone River. From there, the cavalry would mount a massive attack on the Sioux and Northern Cheyenne. The writer of the article hoped their efforts would be "crowned with success" and that the plains would "soon be free of the red vermin that have been so troublesome in recent days to white settlers." The stern-wheeler *Far West*, according to the article, would remain moored on the Yellowstone to supply Custer's troopers and to bring wounded men downstream after the battle.

Sutton read on. The article mentioned the Arikara scout Bloody Knife. He was about to stop reading the article when a name in it caught his eye.

Johnny Loud Thunder.

Sutton dropped his feet to the floor and sat up straight in the chair. He stared at the hated name. The article said that

Johnny Loud Thunder was one of Custer's scouts on the expedition.

Sutton stood up quickly, knocking over the chair as he did so, and threw the paper down on the table. After righting the chair and picking up his Winchester, which still leaned against the wall where he had placed it upon arriving at the house, he went outside. There was no sign of Linden.

Sutton intended to leave but he didn't want to leave without bidding good-by to his friend. Where, he wondered, was the man?

A faint memory drifted through his mind, one connected with Linden and the man named Brock. What was it Brock had said earlier? Something about a stand of timber. That was it—a stand of timber on the north end of Eagan's Flat. Maybe that was where Linden was.

Sutton hurried down the hill to the log house that stood below Linden's and knocked loudly on its door. The door was opened by a man wearing only longjohns.

"I'm a friend of Sam Linden's," Sutton told the man. "I wonder if you could tell me where Eagan's Flat is."

"Sure I can," the man said, easing around Sutton. "See that piece of tableland way off there on the far side of town? That's Eagan's Flat."

"Thanks," Sutton said, and walked swiftly down the hill, carrying his rifle. He skirted the town, crossed Eagan's Flat, and made his way toward the timber on the northern fringe of the tableland. Just before he reached it, Linden strolled out from beneath the trees and, when he saw Sutton coming toward him, hailed him.

Sutton went up to Linden and said, "Sam, I'm leaving."

"No luck in town?"

"None. But in your newspaper—that article about Custer—it named Johnny Loud Thunder as one of Custer's scouts."

"Then, judging by what you told me about that half-breed, Custer's liable to have trouble with more than just the Indians. What the hell happened to you?" Linden suddenly asked, staring at the bruises on Sutton's face and the developing black welt under his left eye.

"I met up with Denton and two of his friends." Sutton grinned.

"Judging by the look of you, maybe it's best you're leaving," Linden observed.

"Denton and his boys won't be bothering me none should I decide to stay on here for a month of Sundays, Sam, I can assure you of that." Sutton's grin faded. "Sam, it was awful good seeing you again and getting to talk over old times with you. I'm real sorry to be pulling out so quick."

"I'm sorry to see you go, Luke. But, considering what you told me about that Loud Thunder fellow, I doubt there's any holding you."

"A block and tackle couldn't, Sam." Sutton held out his hand. As Linden shook it, Sutton said, "I'd like to pay you for my bed and board."

Linden shook his head in dismay. "Luke, when are you ever going to learn that you don't have to be so downright fierce about being independent? When are you going to learn to let a friend be a friend to you?"

"Well, Sam, you know I always like to pay my way."

"Do you happen to remember that big bay mesteño you sold me that time down in Texas?"

"Remember him well. Fine horse. Good wind. Strong, he was."

"You wanted forty dollars for him."

Sutton nodded.

"I was willing to pay you thirty-five and did. Well, it seems safe now to admit that that horse turned out to be worth forty-five, fifty even. So let's call ourselves even, how about it?"

The grin was back on Sutton's face again. He slapped Linden on the back and said, "Best of everything to you, Sam."

"The same to you, Luke."

Sutton turned and recrossed Eagan's Flat. Within minutes he was back in Dustville. He went directly to the livery and asked the farrier, who, tongs in hand was sweating over his forge, if he had any horses for sale.

"One or two maybe," was the man's answer.

"I need a good saddle horse and a pack horse that'll lead easy."

The farrier led him to the rear of the livery. "That sorrel there's a good saddle horse. He'll hold up on the trail." As Sutton stepped into the sorrel's stall and began to run his hands over the horse, the farrier said, "Two stalls down you'll find one that can pack. Small, he is, but sturdy."

After checking the pack horse, Sutton asked the farrier how much he wanted for the animals.

The farrier slammed his hammer down on a cherry-red shoe he was holding in his tongs against his anvil and said, "Fifty dollars for the sorrel, thirty for the other one."

Sutton knew the prices were far too high but he had money in his jeans and no time to price-haggle. "I won't dicker," he told the farrier, handing him several bills he stripped from his roll. "I'll be back soon's I buy the gear and provisions I'll be needing."

He returned to the general store and bought a saddle, bridle, saddlebags and blanket, and provisions.

He carried his purchases back to the livery and had just finished making his horses ready for the trip that lay ahead of them when the farrier appeared and asked him where he was headed.

"Up into Montana Territory," Sutton answered, leading both horses toward the door of the livery.

"Now what might you be expecting to find all the way up there?" the farrier asked, scratching his head.

"Trouble," Sutton replied, and swung into the sorrel's saddle.

CHAPTER 6

The following evening, when the sun had left the sky, Sutton reined in his sorrel and dismounted at the base of a low hill that was covered with lush grass and sprinkled with hackberry trees.

After stripping the gear from his horses, he started a fire. He was frying bacon in a skillet when he sighted a rider skylining himself as he rode along the crest of a hill leading a scrawny pack horse. As Sutton watched, he noted the irregular gait of the rider's horse.

As he continued watching, the horse suddenly pitched forward, threw its rider, and came tumbling down the hill toward Sutton's fire.

Sutton put down the skillet he was holding and leaped to his feet as the horse hit the trunk of a nearby hackberry tree and then struggled to its feet. He raced toward the thrown rider, who lay halfway up the hill, face up, arms flung out on either side of his body.

When he reached the man, Sutton got down on one knee beside him. The man's eyes were closed. His mouth was slightly open. Wisps of the thin gray hair that fringed his nearly bald head stirred slightly in the breeze.

Sutton placed the palm of his right hand on the elderly man's chest. He felt it stir, felt a heartbeat. As he withdrew his hand, the supine man's eyelids fluttered open.

"My word," he whispered, "that was a frightful fall."

"You think you broke anything?" Sutton asked him.

The man sat up and ran his hands over his body and legs. "No, I don't think so. I do hope not."

Sutton helped the man get to his feet. "I'll go get your pack horse." He climbed the hill and, gripping the reins of the horse, which was calmly grazing on the hill's crest, led it back down to where the man who had fallen was brushing his clothes in what Sutton thought was a decidedly fastidious manner.

"My glasses," the man moaned. "I seem to have lost them. My glasses and my hat as well. I'm quite unable to see without my glasses. I wonder, sir, would you be so kind as to look about and see if you can locate them for me?"

Without a word, Sutton turned and headed back up the hill. He found the man's hat easily enough near the top of the hill but it took him some time to find the round gold-rimmed glasses that lay partially hidden in the thick grass.

He descended the hill and handed both glasses and hat to the man, who promptly put them on and then declared, "Thank heaven, my glasses weren't broken! I don't know what I should have done had they been broken, I really do not." He peered through his glasses at Sutton and said, "Sir, I do thank you for your help. Let me introduce myself. My name is Owen Davison." He held out his hand.

Sutton shook it and said, "Luke Sutton. You'd best see to that horse you were riding, Mr. Davison."

"See to my horse?"

Sutton nodded. "He's had a bad fall. You ought to look him over to see if he's banged up in any way."

"He looks fine to me, Mr. Sutton."

"Luke'll do." Sutton pointed to the saddle horse. "That right front leg," he said. "He's favoring it. See how he's standing? He won't put any weight on it."

When Davison did nothing except look perplexed, Sutton went over to the horse and picked up its right front leg, bent its hoof back, and examined its shoe. He called out and beckoned to Davison.

When Davison was standing beside him, he said, "He's got himself a badly bruised sole on account of there's gravel wedged in here in the seat of the shoe. See?"

"No."

Sutton pulled his knife from his boot, unsheathed it, and began to pry the gravel from the seat of the shoe with the knife's blade. Then, using the butt of his .44, he hammered the shoe firmly in place. "He'll be about fine in a day or two. Once that bruising heals."

"Do you live around here, Luke?"

When Sutton got over the surprise Davison's question had elicited in him, he answered, "Nope."

"Neither do I," Davison said cheerfully. "I'm from Connecticut actually. I'm employed there—at Yale University."

"Connecticut," Sutton repeated, stroking his chin and studying Davison. "You're a long way from home. What might you be doing way out here?"

"Well, I'm making my way back to the Badlands," Davison answered, pointing to the west. "I'm afraid I've strayed off course, so to speak."

"Mr. Davison."

"Yes?"

"The Badlands are back that way." Sutton pointed to the southeast.

"I do seem to have lost my bearings, don't I?"

"Looks like you have. What exactly are you planning to do in the Badlands?"

"Well, you see, I'm a paleontologist," Davison said, wiping the beads of sweat that dotted his forehead with a linen handkerchief he took from his pocket.

"I see," Sutton said. He didn't.

"Yes, I've been searching for fossils in the Badlands—a gratifyingly rich source of them, by the way—on assignment from the geology department of Yale University. I'm a professor there. Of paleontology, of course."

"You mean you're hunting up old bones?"

"Not just *any* old bones," Davison said hastily, shaking his head. "Only the bones of long-extinct—prehistoric, as a matter of fact—mammals. Bones of, for example, the entelodont —that was a giant pig once upon a time. Or the dinictis. That particular cat was almost as large as the terrible sabertooth. I'm particularly—indeed, *most*—interested in finding fossils of eohippus."

"Eohippus?"

"Let me show you." Davison tore into his pack and came up with a skull fragment from which the lower jaw was missing. "Isn't it marvelous?"

"Well, it's been picked clean as a whistle, I'll say that."

"The dawn horse!" Davison exclaimed, holding the bony fragment up as if it were a votive offering to some exotic sky deity. "Eohippus first appeared on earth some fifteen million years ago. Then it was a forest dweller, you know, and not much larger than a fox terrier. It had four toes on its front feet and only three on its hind feet. But by the Oligocene pe-

riod it was as large as a collie, and by our own time—*voilà!*"
Davison swept the hand that held the skull fragment toward
his pack horse. "There stands the quite remarkable result of
eohippus' evolution!"

Sutton looked from the skull in Davison's hand to the pack
horse.

"May I join you for supper, Luke?" Davison asked him.
"I'll provide the coffee if that's all right with you and I have
some beans in one of my saddlebags."

"Suits me," Sutton said. He watched Davison replace the
skull fragment in his pack and then walk over to his horse
and open his saddlebag. He was frying bacon when Davison
rejoined him.

"Here we are," Davison said, holding up a cloth sack.
"Beans. If I may use your skillet when you've finished with it,
Luke?"

"You're fixing to *fry* beans?"

Davison nodded absently. He picked up the skillet when
Sutton removed the bacon from it and poured some beans
into it from the sack in his hand. As he held the skillet over
the fire, the beans crackled in the bacon grease and broke
open. He sighed and said, "My dream is to find some fossils—
any remnant, no matter how small will do—of a titanothere.
The Indians, you know, have romanticized the creature most
beautifully. Did you know that, when they first found the
bones of one of those animals which were, when alive, quite
as large as a rhinoceros—they called it Thunderhorse. *Thunderhorse!* A truly wonderful, almost poetic name. These
primitives out here in the West have a way of seeing the
world that is quite impressive, really."

"These primitives, as you call them, Mr. Davison, also have another way of seeing the world—especially white men roaming around in it. It's not a very nice way either. Not the least bit poetic." Sutton hesitated and then asked, "Mr. Davison, would you mind telling me something?"

"What is it you want to know, Luke?"

"Why aren't you carrying a rifle? Or at least a sidearm of some sort?"

"Oh, I'm certain that no Indian would want to harm me. A paleontologist is certainly no threat to them. But if I were to carry a—what did you call it?"

"A sidearm."

"Yes, a sidearm, to be sure. If I had a sidearm—or a rifle—why, the Indians might think I meant them harm. This way, without weapons, I needn't expect any trouble from them."

"Your beans are burning," Sutton said, shaking his head and pointing to the skillet from which smoke was rising.

When Sutton awoke the next morning, a dense fog rolled silently along the ground at the base of the hill, hiding its crest from sight. Wiping the fog's moisture from his face, he threw off his blanket and got up. He bent down and picked up his Smith and Wesson, which had been beneath the blanket beside him during the night, and holstered it. He squinted into the fog and was barely able to make out the indistinct forms of his two horses, which he had picketed on the side of the hill before going to sleep the night before.

He looked down at the still sleeping Davison, who was almost completely hidden from sight beneath a huge fur coat he had taken from his pack before bedding down for the night. A glance to his left told Sutton that Davison's horses were still tied to the hackberry tree where the man had left them for the night.

Moving through the fog, Sutton went to his horses, unpicketed his pack horse, and led it back to the campsite, where he proceeded to load it with his gear.

He turned swiftly as he felt a hand land on his shoulder, reaching for his .44 as he did so.

Davison drew back in alarm. His mouth fell open.

"You come up behind a man the way you just did, Mr. Davison, you might get yourself shot," Sutton said angrily.

"I am sorry, Luke. I didn't mean to startle you. But, you see, I woke up and I said to myself, Owen, you never did express your thanks to Luke for fixing your saddle horse's shoe yesterday."

"I was glad to do it," Sutton said, relaxing.

"I say, Luke, are you getting ready to travel on?"

"I am. I'll be riding out right after breakfast."

"Breakfast," Davison repeated. "We'll need a good fire, won't we? I'll gather some wood."

As Davison scampered up the side of the hill, Sutton continued tying his gear on his horse. When he finished the task, he turned to find Davison kneeling beside a fire he had made which was sending up more smoke than flame. The smoke made Sutton uneasy and he went over to the fire, intending to kick it out and start a smaller one.

But when he reached the fire, Davison, on his knees, looked up at him, smiled happily, and said, "A nice fire, isn't it? It does take away the chill this fog has brought with it."

"The air does have a nip to it," Sutton said, and coughed as the breeze blew smoke into his face.

"I'll cook our breakfast," Davison volunteered.

Sutton hunkered downwind of the fire and watched Davison juggle the skillet, a slab of bacon, a pocket knife, and several pieces of hardtack.

Half an hour later he took the plate Davison handed him and proceeded to eat the rigid strips of bacon that were on it. He chewed some hardtack, thinking of the skull fragment Davison had shown him. He found himself wondering if Davison would get out of the Black Hills and the Badlands in any better shape than had that ancient horse to whom the skull had belonged.

"Which way are you traveling, Luke?"

"Northwest."

"For what reason, if I may be so bold as to inquire?"

"I plan on joining up with General Custer and his Seventh Cavalry."

"So you're a soldier! I knew it! You have the look of a military man about you."

"Mr. Davison, I'm not a . . ."

"It shows in your eyes—they're so keen. And in the way you have of looking at a man—appraising him very coolly and clearly. It shows as well in the way you carry yourself. Easy—but alert and with a look on your face that declares you are ready for anything. Do you plan to fight Indians with General Custer?"

"Not exactly." Just one half-Indian, Sutton thought grimly.

"I'd never make a good military man myself even if I were very much younger," Davison mused. "No, the scholar's life is the one for me. I fight the battles of the mind, you might say. Of course, mine is a pale life compared with yours, Luke."

"Well, I'm not so certain of that, Mr. Davison. There are lots of things in books that I know I could never win a battle against where you, no doubt, could."

"But you are obviously a man of action, Luke. You're at home here in the wilderness. Oh, I've been watching you, so I know. I dare say that you, unlike me, can cope with just about everything that befalls you. I, on the other hand, have been known, at home in Connecticut, to appear in public wearing socks that don't match. Perhaps you see what I mean."

"Mismatched socks don't make you any the less of a professor though, I'm willing to bet."

"Well, I suppose that's true enough. Still, I think you know what I mean about us—our differences. I admire—can't help but admire—a man like yourself who can—well, *do* things.

"When I was a boy," Davison continued thoughtfully, "I was always fascinated with history—with the past. I rather hate to admit that my fascination with the past was a form of escapism, since I was not very good at playing boys' games nor, later, at courting girls. I read every history book I could get my hands on. For a time I longed to have lived in the golden age of Pericles in ancient Athens. I imagined myself at times as a privy counselor to the Bourbon kings." Davison paused, his eyes on the ground. "It's really no wonder, obsessed as I was with the past, that I became a paleontologist." He looked up at Sutton and asked, "What about you, Luke? What were you like as a boy?"

Sutton thought about the question for a moment and then said, "Ma was wont to say I was first cousin to mischief. She sometimes said that if there was trouble traveling within ten miles of me I'd be sure to find it without hardly even looking for it. I just seemed to have a natural attraction to it. Took to it like a duck takes to water, she used to say."

"And what did you want to be when you grew up?"

Sutton pondered Davison's question and then said, "Nothing special that I can recall. All I really ever wanted to be was a lot like my Pa once I was grown. Now there was a thunderer of a man! My Pa, he was good with a gun, even better with dumb critters. My brother had a book I looked into once when we were boys. It had this picture in it of a man—big as a mountain he was—all stooped over and holding up the earth on his back." Sutton paused, frowning.

"Atlas," Davison said.

"There you go!" Sutton said. "That was the man's name all right. He reminded me of my Pa, that Atlas did. I used to tell myself that if that Atlas fellow ever got tired, why, Pa could spell him just about any old time at all.

"Pa, after he'd brought Ma and my brother and me West from Tennessee, built our homeplace with his own hands and too little help from us boys, who were always off larking somewhere. He farmed, did some cowboying from time to time, taught me and my brother to ride, shoot, trap, skin, and make do with whatever was our lot in life. He was a real good man, my Pa was." Sutton paused again and then added, "I reckon all I ever wanted to be was just a whole lot like him."

"An admirable ambition, judging by what you've just told me about him," Davison said softly, pushing his glasses up on his nose.

"Well, now, I don't know. I didn't mention that Pa had a real strong thirst for whiskey that got the better of him now and then. And Ma once said he had turned the heads and tumbled the hearts of every girl in Tennessee and on up into Kentucky before they were married."

Davison laughed heartily.

Sutton grinned. "Well, I guess I'd better clean up here and be on my way."

"And I must make my way back to the Badlands," Davison said. "I'm sorry we're not traveling in the same direction, Luke. It has been a real pleasure to have had your company."

"I thank you, Mr. Davison. Maybe we'll meet up again sometime."

The fog had lifted while the two men talked and was almost completely gone by the time Sutton had finished packing his gear.

As he stepped into the saddle, Davison came up to him and said, "Awfully sorry to bother you again, Luke. But the Badlands—which way did you say they were?"

Sutton pointed southeast.

"Thank you. Well, I hope you'll have a good journey, Luke."

"You too, Mr. Davison," Sutton said, and watched the man walk toward his saddle horse. He was about to call out to him but instead got out of the saddle and went over to put out the fire that Davison had apparently forgotten about.

Davison's sudden cry of alarm caused Sutton to spin around, his hand going for his .44.

"Don't touch it!" roared a mounted man who was holding a carbine on Sutton.

Sutton's right hand hung motionless in the air inches away from his gun butt. He met the icy gaze of the mounted man, who was sitting his horse in the distance, and then he turned his attention to the other mounted man stationed to the right of the first one.

That man, Sutton saw, also had a carbine in his hands. But it was not aimed at him. It was aimed directly at the spluttering Davison, who was waving his arms in the air as if he were trying to drive the two men from the campsite with his ineffectual gestures.

"Unleather it!" barked the man holding his carbine on Sutton.

Sutton slowly drew his .44 from its holster. For an instant he considered trying to get off a shot. He might, he thought, bring down the nearer of the two men. But the other might get Davison before he could fire a second time. He held the gun out in front of him.

"Throw it my way!" the man ordered.

Sutton drew his arm back and, when he thought the gun was out of the man's line of sight, he cocked it and hurled it toward the man.

When it hit the ground, the hammer slammed down as Sutton had hoped it would and, as the shot ripped through the air, Sutton raced toward the man who had given him the order and whose horse had reared at the sound of the shot.

He managed to leap up and grab the barrel of the man's carbine before the second man let out an angry yell and Sutton saw that the man had him in his sights. He released the carbine's barrel and stepped away from the still fidgeting horse.

Now both carbines were aimed at him.

He put up his hands.

"Tricky bastard, aren't you?" barked the man Sutton had jumped.

"Just one moment, please!" Davison called out, moving toward the man who had spoken to Sutton.

Without taking his eyes from Sutton, the man said to his partner, "Old duffer, ain't he, Markham?" The man was obviously referring to Davison.

"Pops is pushing close to a hundred sure," Markham said and giggled.

"I say!" Davison exclaimed as he came around to stand beside Sutton. "Just what is it you two gentlemen mean by riding in here with your guns and foul language?"

Markham said, "Tell him, Thorne."

Thorne shook his head, his eyes still riveted on Sutton. "Not now. We'll surprise these two. More fun that way."

Markham's high-pitched giggle sounded again and then there was silence for a moment.

Davison broke it. "This is outrageous!" he cried, shaking a small fist at Thorne, his face flushing. "We've done you no harm . . ."

"And aren't likely to do us any!" Thorne said.

"What do you want?" Davison asked him. "Money? I have very little but what I have you're welcome to take if you'll just leave here—leave us alone."

"We'll take it," Thorne assured him.

"Quite a haul we made this time," Markham commented gleefully. "Four horses. A whole lot of gear. Two men. Well, one anyway," he amended, nodding in Sutton's direction. "What do you think we ought to do with this other old one, Thorne?"

"He's frail," Thorne said with a wink at Markham. "Awful old and real frail."

"See here!" Davison sputtered.

Thorne raised a booted foot and slammed it against Davison's face.

The old man teetered back, blood streaming down his face, his spectacles shattered and hanging from one ear.

Sutton caught him before he could fall and eased him to the ground. He knelt beside him.

"My glasses," Davison murmured thickly, reaching for them.

"They're broken, Mr. Davison," Sutton said softly.

"Broken," Davison repeated. His fingers touched his equally broken lips and he winced. "I'm practically *blind* without them," he cried, "and they're the only pair I have, Luke!"

"I guess that sort of settles it, don't it, Thorne?" Markham asked.

"It does," Thorne replied. "He's no good to us blind. No good at all."

Sutton threw himself backward at the sound of Thorne's shot. Thorne's bullet slammed into Davison's body, causing it to lurch violently. Davison's blood spattered Sutton's shirt as it erupted from the hole that had been torn in his throat.

As Sutton looked up at Thorne, Thorne fired a second time.

Markham giggled.

Thorne's bullet had entered Davison's chest. His third shot widened the hole made by his second.

Sutton clenched his teeth as he got to his feet, staring up at Thorne. And then, in a low voice, he said, "You're mighty profligate with your ammunition, Thorne, seeing as how you killed that old man with your first shot."

"Thorne," Markham said, "is a man who likes to make sure of things."

"String those horses together!" Thorne shouted to him.

"Your friend," Sutton said to Thorne as Markham dismounted and began to go through Davison's pockets, "says you like to make certain of things. Well, Thorne, you'd best make certain you keep your eyes on me. You don't, you so much as blink, and I'll kill you."

"A careless gent like you's not likely to do any killing," Thorne countered. "Anybody dumb enough to build a smoky fire like the one you made which put us on to you in the first place—I'm not much worried about getting killed by the likes of you."

Sutton looked down at Davison's ravaged corpse. "What do you have in mind to do with me?" he asked Thorne, his eyes on Davison's shattered spectacles.

"I'll tell you this much," Thorne answered. "You're going to be put to work. Hard work it is, too. But that shouldn't bother a strong young buck like you."

"What kind of work?" Sutton asked, looking up into Thorne's tight face in which the man's black eyes glittered.

"You'll find out soon enough," Thorne told him. He glanced at Markham and yelled, "You ready to move out?"

"Sure am!" Markham called back.

Thorne gestured with his carbine in Sutton's direction. "You walk on ahead where I can keep both eyes on you like you recommended I do." To Markham, he called out, "Get the gun that this new employee of ours was carrying. It's right down there in the grass." He looked down at Sutton. "I heard the old duffer call you Luke. Luke what?"

"Sutton."

"Move out, Sutton!"

"The old man," Sutton said. "He deserves a proper burying."

Thorne barked his order a second time.

Sutton moved out.

"Not that way!" Thorne bellowed at him. "*North!*"

Sutton turned and headed north.

Behind him rode Thorne and Markham, their carbines aimed at his back.

CHAPTER 7

Sutton had walked less than a mile when Thorne ordered him to halt. He stopped but didn't turn toward his captors.

"What's wrong, Thorne?" he heard Markham ask and Thorne answer, "Nothing. Just had me an idea though. I'm more than willing to turn these horses and their gear over to Kirby—we'll get our share of them. But I was thinking . . ."

"What were you thinking?" Markham asked Thorne.

"I'll keep this carbine on Sutton. You get off of that horse and take his cartridge belt. Make him empty out his pockets."

When Markham appeared in front of him, Sutton, knowing that Thorne and his carbine were behind him, unstrapped his cartridge belt without a word and handed it to the grinning Markham.

"Now your pockets," Markham said. "Empty 'em out on the ground."

Sutton thrust both hands into his pockets and pulled them inside out. His roll of bills, loose change, his makeshift snakeskin sling, and his flint and steel fell to the ground.

"*Whooeee!*" Markham shouted, and then he was on his hands and knees scrambling after the money that was being blown about by the breeze. "Money!" he yelled to Thorne. "*Lots of it!*" When he had gathered up all the bills and the

change, he counted it and looked over Sutton's shoulder at
Thorne. "There's hundreds here!"

"We'll go half and half on it," Thorne said. "What old
Black Jack Kirby don't know won't hurt him none."

Markham dropped from sight behind Sutton and Sutton
heard the two men dividing up his money. He heard Thorne
say, "Nice gun he's got. New belt and holster. I'll keep them
and his rifle and saddle for myself."

Markham said something Sutton didn't hear.

"What are you going to do about your objection?" Thorne
shot at him. When Markham didn't reply, Thorne ordered
Sutton to move on.

He did.

He estimated that he had covered three, possibly four,
more miles when, after rounding a ridge, he spotted a stockade in the distance. As he came closer to it, he could see that
it was built of twenty-five-foot logs that measured two to three
feet in diameter. They were hewn square and placed so close
together that he could not see what might be inside the
stockade.

To the right of it was a corral. Sutton counted fourteen
horses in it.

As he walked on, he heard the sound of hammering. It was
coming, he believed, from behind the stockade.

"Around to the left," Thorne called out to him.

Sutton made his way around the left side of the stockade,
noting the tall platforms that had been built at intervals outside its walls. When he reached the far end of the stockade
wall, he saw the source of the hammering. At least a dozen
men of assorted sizes and ages were using sledge hammers to

pulverize what appeared to Sutton to be several tons of quartz that was heaped in a high pile near them.

To his right and just beyond the laborers was a log cabin. Smoke rose from its chimney. Scattered about behind it were numerous army tents, their canvas flaps flipping in the wind. Guarding the men with the sledges were two men armed with Springfield rifles.

"Head on up to that cabin, Sutton!" Thorne ordered. "Markham, strip those horses and corral them. You can toss Sutton's saddle and other gear inside my tent."

Markham nodded and wheeled his horse. Sutton walked on, Thorne riding right behind him, and, when he reached the cabin, he halted.

Thorne dismounted and, keeping his carbine trained on Sutton, went up to the cabin door and knocked on it.

"Yeah?" a male voice inside the cabin yelled.

"Kirby, we got ourselves a new employee. I figured you'd want to tell him a thing or two about how we do here."

A moment later the cabin door swung outward and a tall man with a black beard stepped out, brushed past Thorne, and stood before Sutton, his legs spread and his booted feet planted firmly on the ground. He looked Sutton up and down and then, folding his arms over his chest, he said, "This is my mining camp. We do gold mining here. I'm Kirby. Some call me Black Jack Kirby 'cause I've been a gambling man in my time."

Sutton decided that Kirby was not very much older than he was. The man's features were coarse, his beard matted. A ragged line of scar tissue ran down his neck from his left ear.

"Thorne and Markham are my scouts," Kirby continued.

"They find me workers the way they found you. You a good worker? What do they call you, mister?"

"Sutton."

"Well?" Kirby prompted, unfolding his arms and planting his hands on his hips. "I asked you if you're a good worker."

"I've done hard work."

"Good. That's real good because you're going to find out and find out fast that the work here is hard. It's gut-busting work. That's why I set up this operation of mine the way I did. First off, I found some color over there in Deep Creek. I was panning on my own then. I worked my way upstream and found a blowup. It looked to be a rich vein and I hacked away at that blossom rock till I was about ready to drop. It turned out to be a real rich lode all right.

"But then I had me a problem I had to sort out. No bank anywhere would lend a man like me the kind of money I'd need to buy drills or a stamping mill to crush ore. I was stymied. But then along came another bunch of prospectors—more respectable ones—if you know what I mean. They offered to buy me out. But I'm a stubborn man and I wouldn't sell."

Markham appeared and took up a position next to Sutton.

"I had me an idea then," Kirby continued. "Rounded me up some hard cases—my apologies, Thorne, Markham—and made them a proposition. They rounded up some of their friends and acquaintances and then they went to work rounding up strays like yourself who were hightailing it around the Hills and we put them to work in my mine. First, of course, we had them build that stockade back there. Then we got us supplies—sledges and shovels and such. Even hired a cook.

"I take seventy-five per cent of what you men mine for me. My boys split the other twenty-five per cent among themselves. They eat free. They sleep in tents I bought for them. So, for them, it's not a bad life. But you and my other laborers have to make do as best you can in the stockade."

"Your slave laborers," Sutton amended.

Kirby swiftly slapped Sutton's face, first with his palm, and then he backhanded him.

Sutton lunged forward, reaching out for Kirby, and was jumped by Markham, who pinioned his arms behind him, tripped him, and brought him to his knees.

"First thing you got to learn," Kirby said, looking down at Sutton, "is not to sass your betters."

"I never have done that," Sutton said.

Kirby reached down and seized Sutton's chin in his huge right hand. He squeezed until Sutton was sure his jaw was about to crack. "Smart, huh? Think you are?"

Sutton stared up into Kirby's angry eyes.

Kirby released him. "This one," he said, pointing at Sutton, "is going to need a whole lot of breaking before he can be harnessed."

"I'll delight in doing the breaking," Thorne said enthusiastically. "I most surely will."

"See those perches up there on top of the stockade walls?" Kirby asked Sutton. When he received no reply, he said, "When you laborers are all locked up at night, we put guards up there on those perches. Guards with good guns. Anybody tries to escape—my boys have orders to shoot to kill."

Sutton shook himself free of Markham, who was still holding him, and rose to his feet.

Kirby said, "Put him to work crushing quartz for a start." He turned and went back into his cabin, slamming the door behind him.

"You heard him, Sutton." Thorne nudged Sutton in the ribs with the barrel of his carbine.

Sutton turned and started walking toward the small mountain of quartz where the men, under the wary eyes of their two guards, were swinging their sledges.

When he reached it, he bent down and picked up a fourteen-pound sledge that was lying on the ground. He swung it over his head and brought it down hard on a boulder of quartz, splitting it into fragments in which flecks of gold sparkled in the sunlight. He swung the sledge again and again brought it down, pulverizing several of the fragments.

A prisoner who looked to be no more than sixteen appeared among the men with a bucket into which he scooped crumbled quartz. When his bucket was filled, he headed back the way he had come.

As Sutton's sledge struck again, he asked the man working next to him where the boy was going.

"Deep Creek," was the muttered answer. "Him and some others pan this stuff down at the creek."

Sutton worked on, his sledge rising and falling rhythmically, the noise of his own and that of the other sledges resounding in the air.

Before an hour had passed, he took off his hat and dropped it on the ground at his feet. He untied his bandana and made a headband with it to catch the sweat that was streaming into his eyes.

He worked on, his blue shirt dark with sweat. But he

didn't remove it as he was tempted to do. He had seen the sun-blistered flesh of two shirtless men working near him.

"Where's this mine of Kirby's?" he asked the man working beside him.

"Just hope you don't find out," the man answered.

Sutton asked his question of the man working on his opposite side.

"Up around that ridge over there. That's where the entrance to the main shaft is. But the spur tunnels spread out in all directions. Even underneath us here where we stand and labor so joyously." The man's voice was bitter, tired.

Sutton let his sledge come to rest on the ground. He stretched and rubbed the small of his back, staring at the ridge in the distance. As he rested, several carts pulled by mules came into view from behind the ridge. When they reached the laboring men, their drivers began to unload more quartz from the carts.

Sutton felt the muzzle of a gun in his back.

"Don't turn around," someone behind him said. "Just put that hammer into the air and keep it moving."

Sutton rolled his shoulders to loosen his muscles and then raised his sledge hammer. The muzzle of the gun was removed from his back.

"It'll soon be sundown," he said much later to the man working at his side. "How long are we expected to keep this up?"

"Till about sundown. If we make our quota."

"And if we don't?"

"It's a lot cooler working in the moonlight."

Sutton estimated that the sun had been below the horizon

for nearly an hour when he heard one of the guards yell, "Fall in!"

He dropped his sledge hammer, pulled his bandana from his head and pocketed it, and then picked up his hat and put it on. He joined the ragged double column the prisoners were wearily forming.

"Move out!" the same guard shouted, and the column of men began to shuffle toward the stockade.

Sutton glanced back over his shoulder and saw more men rounding the ridge, evidently coming from the mine, their faces caked with dirt.

The stockade gate stood open and, as Sutton went through it, he could not believe what he saw. The acres of hard-packed grassless ground which were enclosed by the four walls of the stockade were littered with human filth. Here and there men had tried to construct shelters made of clothing or torn canvas laid over branches or barrel staves.

Once inside the gate, the double column dissolved. Men moved off in all directions. One or two just slumped to the ground where they stood. One man crawled beneath what Sutton recognized as having once been a blanket. He stepped to one side, surveying the scene before him.

The stockade walls, he thought, might be climbable. But the guards on their perches—well, he told himself, men get sleepy and in the dark . . .

If he could get his hands on a shovel . . . He wondered how deeply the logs had been set in the ground.

A man stumbled against him and Sutton lost his balance. The man who had stumbled against him grabbed Sutton and pulled him away from the rope barrier that was several yards away from the stockade walls and ran parallel to them.

"You new to this place, so you maybe don't know that

there's the dead line," the man said to Sutton. "You put so much as your big toe over it, white man, and *whammo!* You shot dead."

"I'm obliged for the information," Sutton told the bare-footed black man who stood beside him swaying slightly, clad only in torn trousers that were too short for him.

"Some mens try to escape from here last year," the man said. "So the guards put up that there dead line. You step over it, they figure—they *like* to figure—you planning to climb up the wall and so they shoot at you. They don't never miss neither." The man's body listed and his legs seemed about to give out on him.

Sutton reached out, grabbed one of the man's arms, and threw it over his shoulder. "You got a special place that's yours in here?" he asked.

"They don't allow me none, being a Negro like I am."

"You want to sit down here?"

"Here's about as good a place as the next," the man said. Looking down at the ground, he added, "Least this one's near clean."

Sutton eased the man to the ground and then sat down beside him. A winged maggot landed on Sutton's hand and he crushed the insect against his jeans. "Pesky things," he growled.

"I sure enough can testify to that," said the man beside him. He pointed to his right foot.

Sutton stared at the man's foot, trying to suppress the disgust that churned within him.

The black flesh had been eaten away to expose most of the bones in the man's foot. White maggots were devouring the man's flesh as they squirmed in the red cavity.

"That's how they do start out," the man said tonelessly,

looking down at his ravaged flesh. "Then they sprout some wings and set out to see a piece of the world."

"What happened?" Sutton asked.

"I had me a hat when I first come in here," the man answered. "Fell off, it did, one day some time back. I reached over the dead line to where it had rolled and one of the guards, he shot me in the foot."

"What have you been doing for it?"

"All I can, which amounts to mostly nothing."

"Don't they have any kind of medicine here? Kirby must have some means of keeping you—us—healthy."

The black man laughed. "Mr. Kirby, he as tight with two bits as he is with a dollar. That means old Noah here's got hisself some big kind of trouble a-racing up the road after him."

"I can see that," Sutton said, unable to take his eyes from the feeding maggots whose pale bodies were flecked with Noah's blood.

Noah shook his head. "No, sir, you sure enough can't see my meaning. What I'm meaning is Carew."

"Carew?"

"Carew been here even longer than me and I in somewhat over a year now. Carew, he the white man what does the picking and choosing."

"I don't follow you, Noah. By the way, my name's Luke."

"What I aiming to explain to you, Luke, is that this here Carew, now he come round every morning when we be marched out of here and he decide then who is fit and who ain't fit to work. Those what are, they go on off to work. Those Carew say ain't, they go to glory."

"You mean he . . ."

"He shoot the misfit mens and has them hauled off somewheres. Kirby says it no use to feed mens who can't work. And I sure won't be fit much longer, what with all these worms eating me alive so I can't hardly stand up no more."

Sutton got to his feet and yelled up to a guard.

The guard simply stared down at him.

"This man needs care!" Sutton yelled, pointing at Noah.

The guard continued to stare in silence at Sutton.

"Give me something to kill the maggots in his foot!" Sutton yelled. When the guard still did not respond, he yelled, "Kirby won't like it if you let Carew kill a man who can pull his share of the load if only his foot's looked after."

Sutton's ploy worked. The guard turned and called down to someone on the other side of the stockade.

Sutton waited.

"It best not to make a fuss," Noah said to him in a breathless whisper. "Don't do to go calling attention to yourself. Best way to get along inside here is to be invisible." He laughed harshly. "That a real hard thing for a Negro man like me to be."

The guard leaned over the log wall and tossed a bottle down to Sutton, who caught it and then dropped down on the ground beside Noah. He unstoppered the bottle and held it to his nose. "I asked for some kind of medicine," he muttered to himself, "and he hands me this!"

"What it, Luke?"

"Turpentine."

"Better than nothing," Noah said philosophically. "Might be it can kill these worms that are killing me little bit by little bit."

"But your wound—it's all raw."

Noah nodded. "I know what you be getting around to. I'll suffer the sting best as I can."

Sutton poured a thin stream of turpentine from the bottle on the maggots.

Noah cried out in agony as the turpentine scalded his raw flesh, his head thrown back, his hands gripping his leg just above his ankle.

A mass of worms flopped to the ground, still squirming.

"Once more, Noah?" Sutton asked.

Noah gritted his teeth and nodded. When the turpentine seared his flesh again, he opened his mouth and screamed.

Sutton pulled his bandana from his pocket and began to wipe from Noah's wound the few maggots that remained in it. When he looked up, Noah's face was contorted, and from his eyes, which he had squeezed shut, tears oozed.

"I'm real sorry, Noah."

Noah opened his eyes. "No call for you to be sorry, Luke. Them worms is all gone."

"I know it hurt bad," Sutton said, stoppering the bottle and placing it on the ground beside him.

"*Kill him!*" someone screamed from the far side of the stockade.

Men began moving toward the spot where the shout had come from.

A crowd soon formed, and then out of it strode a tall man who was holding another man by the scruff of the neck. "He stole my tin cup!" the tall man bellowed to the crowd.

"Whup him good!" someone in the crowd shouted back.

And then—silence.

Sutton saw the tall man force his captive to bend forward. The man, doubled over, gripped his ankles in both hands.

The tall man reached out and pulled the man's pants halfway down his thighs. Someone in the crowd handed the tall man a long strip of leather that Sutton recognized as having once been part of a saddle's latigo. He watched as the tall man savagely whipped the bare buttocks of his prisoner.

Noah said, "That white man ain't likely to keep thieving now."

As Noah was speaking, the stockade gate swung open and three men carrying drawn six-guns entered the stockade. Behind them, driven by a fourth man, came a mule-drawn wagon.

"Supper," Noah said, nodding in the direction of the wagon.

"That's an odd sort of chuck wagon," Sutton commented. "You have a mess kit of some kind that I can share, Noah?"

Noah shook his head sadly. "Not many mens in here have such a thing. That why that tall fellow made such a fuss about his tin cup being thieved."

Men were moving toward the wagon, which had stopped just inside the gate. One stumbled, fell, got to his feet, and held onto the wagon for support.

"You best move out smart, Luke," Noah advised, "if you want to get your share of supper."

"I got nothing at all I can use to eat from."

"That sets you to sail in the same boat as most of the rest of us. Some mens use their hands. Fingers was invented before forks, they say. See that fellow over there at the wagon?"

"The one pulling off his boot, you mean?"

"Watch what he do."

Sutton saw the man use his boot to scoop up some of whatever was in the wagon bed. He saw another man use a lopsided bowl that had been made from the bark of a tree in the same manner.

"Noah, you coming? Can you make it?"

"I just going to sit here and rest a spell."

Sutton studied Noah, who avoided his gaze, his head lowered, his hands resting idly in his lap. Then he turned and went toward the wagon.

When he reached it, he discovered that the wooden wagon bed was filled with a thin mush that looked like it might have been made from corn meal. He glanced back at Noah, who was watching him. Then, elbowing aside the men on either side of him, he moved in close to the wagon and, taking off his hat, he filled it with mush, which he carried back to where Noah was still sitting.

"Here," he said, handing Noah his hat. "You go first."

Noah, gripping Sutton's hat by the brim in both hands, raised it to his lips. Some of the watery gruel slid down his chin as he poured it into his mouth. A moment later he offered the hat to Sutton.

"Have some more," Sutton said, and Noah lifted the hat to his lips a second time.

Then, accepting his hat from Noah, Sutton consumed the mush that remained in it. "They surely don't dote on cleanliness around here, now do they?" he commented, scouring the inside of his hat with his fingers and then licking them clean. "Dumping mush in a wagon bed! Why, I've seen hogs slopped better."

"The rations don't be so good nowadays," Noah commented. "Once though—it were just before winter set in last year—we had us some apples. Fine they was, fine and sweet and, oh my, so *juicy!* I still sometimes remember those apples and my mouth waters like a river in flood."

"Kirby keeps his prisoners in here all winter without any shelter?"

"He do. It get awful cold sometimes. When snow come, some of the white mens huddle up with each other to keep warm. Some of them, they prance about to keep their bloods on the move. But winter, it do take its toll. Mens lose toes—fingers too—all frostbit bad. Toes ain't so bad but fingers—a man can't work his best without all ten of his fingers, and then once he loses a couple, along comes Carew with his six-shooter."

"How many men have died since you been here, Noah?"

"A dozen, more or less."

"Only a dozen? I'd have thought there would have been more, considering." Sutton waved his hand to encompass the stockade.

"Luke, you ask me how many mens *died.* If you was to ask me how many Carew shot to death, I have to say more like thirty, forty."

Sutton let out a low whistle. He watched the wagon driver turn the wagon. As the man drove it out through the gate, the gate was closed behind it and Sutton heard a heavy bar drop into place on its far side.

"It too bad those mens catched you, Luke," Noah said, wiping his lips with the back of his hand.

"I can see now that it surely was too bad. I can also see why they send out scouts. These men in here are in real poor physical condition, most of them. Kirby must need to replace the ones that—die—at a great rate."

"Oh, he do. But he don't have no recruiting problem. You seen how his scouts do." Noah was lost in thought for a moment and then he said, "When I first got put in here, I never hoped to last long as I have. This here an awful lot worse'n the cavalry ever was."

"You were in the cavalry?" Sutton sat down on the ground next to Noah after making sure he was far enough away from the dead line to avoid drawing fire from the guards.

"Tenth Cavalry Regiment was mine," Noah said. "Us fought Indians all over the plains. Specially Apaches."

"The Tenth was an all-Negro regiment, wasn't it?"

"We one of but four in the whole entire United States Cavalry," Noah answered with unconcealed pride.

"I heard you boys could fight as mean as any Apache and even longer if need be."

Noah looked at Sutton, saw his grin, and smiled. "Us buffalo soldiers did mostly hold our own. I do wish I was out on the plains fighting Apaches right now. I truly do. Should've re-enlisted. But I went and caught me a case of gold fever and headed for the Hills. Lord, just look at where my gold fever got me!"

The two men talked on as dusk deepened into darkness, and then Noah stretched out on the ground, carefully placing his wounded foot on top of his good one and pillowing his head with his hands.

Lanterns were lighted and hung on the guards' perches. They shed a flickering light over the huddled forms that lay everywhere on the ground inside the stockade.

Sutton stretched out on his back and, with his hands clasped behind his head, stared up at the stars, not seeing them, thinking of escape, and later, when he slept, he dreamed of tunnels that went down deep into the earth and then came out in a field of primrose through which flowed a stream in which he washed the sweat and grime from his body and the memory of Black Jack Kirby's stockade from his mind.

In the morning when he awoke, Sutton found Noah sitting by his side and staring steadily at the stockade's gate.

"You waiting for the chuck wagon?" Sutton asked.

"We get only a meal a day in here," Noah replied without taking his eyes from the gate.

Sutton noted the stiffness of Noah's body.

"What's wrong?" he asked, and guessed even before Noah answered him by saying simply, "Carew."

"You can lean on me as we go through the gate," Sutton told him. "Throw your left arm over my shoulder. You can hop along that way, can't you?"

"I daren't."

"Why not?"

"Daren't let Carew see I'm lame so bad."

At that moment the gate swung open. A guard yelled from his perch, "*Move out, louts!*"

Sutton stood up and then reached down to help Noah get to his feet. "Get behind me, Noah," he said. "Get up real close and put your hands on my shoulders. Where exactly does Carew stand to check us over?"

"He stand right outside the gate," Noah said with a sigh.

"Let's go," Sutton said, helping Noah limp over to the slowly forming double column that had begun shambling toward the open gate, flanked by guards with drawn guns.

Both men got in line and Sutton, looking over his shoulder, muttered, "Grab hold of me, Noah. Grit your teeth and walk as sound as you can until we reach Carew. Then let go and do the best you can. Once we're past Carew, you can get a good grip on my shoulders again."

"He see you trying to help me, Luke, that Carew'll do for me and you both for sure. Mean, he is. Awful mean white man, that Carew."

"*Do as I say!*" Sutton snapped. When he felt Noah grip his shoulders, he moved forward slowly toward the gate.

A moment later he whispered, "Here we are, Noah. Now you let go, hear, and you do your damnedest!" He glanced at the man who was standing in apparent idleness to the right of the gate just outside the stockade, eyes alert as if he were watching a Fourth of July parade.

Sutton suddenly halted.

"Luke!" Noah muttered. "That *him!* That Carew standing off to the right."

Sutton took a step forward and then another, his eyes on the man Noah had identified. He wanted to reach out and smash that face with both of his fists. He did nothing because he didn't want to call attention to Noah's lameness.

"That one!" the man Sutton was watching called out, pointing at a man not far ahead of Sutton who was stumbling along with his head drooping.

A guard flanking the column reached out and pulled the man from the line.

"No!" the man cried, springing suddenly to alarmed life. "Not me, please, Carew! I'm still strong. I *am!* I . . ."

"You're skinny as a telegraph wire and as weak as a just-foaled colt to boot. You can't hardly lift a sledge hammer, let alone swing one!"

Sutton saw the man draw his Colt and shoot the man who had been pulled from the column at close range, blasting away half of his face.

"Move on!" a guard shouted to the column of men filing slowly along.

As Sutton moved on, he felt Noah's hands leave his shoulders. Moments later they again gripped Sutton's shoulders.

Noah whispered, "We got us by that Carew just fine! Oh my, didn't we do that real slick though?"

"You! Nigger!"

Sutton felt Noah's hands slide from his shoulders. He heard Noah say, "Mr. Carew, I is just a little bit . . ."

"Thought I didn't spot you, didn't you, nigger? But that foot of yours is mighty hard to miss. It left a real clear trail of blood behind you. Step out of line, nigger, if you *can* still step with but one foot fit to stand up on."

"Mr. Carew, sir, I can . . ."

"You know damned well you can't work and I know it too!"

Sutton turned as a shot sounded. He saw Noah fall to the ground and lie there shuddering as blood drained from the exit wound a bullet had made in his bare back. Sutton stared at the man standing over Noah, a smoking Colt in his hand, and said, "So you call yourself Carew these days. But you were calling yourself Adam Foss that night two years ago in Texas when you shot me and helped kill my brother. Foss, you listen up! You got away from me once after that in Dodge City. You won't get away from me again."

"*Sutton!*" Foss exclaimed, his eyes wide, his voice barely audible. He stepped backward.

"I'm going to kill you, Foss!" Sutton said, taking a step toward him.

"*Guard!*" Foss yelled, quickly moving out of Sutton's reach. "Get this man back into line!"

A guard appeared and shoved Sutton back into line.

He moved forward with the rest of the prisoners, looking back over his shoulder at the man who went by the name of Carew—the man he knew as Adam Foss.

CHAPTER 8

Sutton cursed himself for what he had done as he swung his sledge hammer to pulverize the quartz boulders covering the ground around him.

He should have kept his mouth shut, he told himself. He should not have confronted Foss. What he should have done, he now believed, was to keep Foss from even noticing him. But now that Foss had seen him, he realized, his life was in danger. He was sure that Foss would take the first opportunity that presented itself to kill him. And here no one would ask any questions about why Foss had shot one more slave laborer.

But he hadn't been able to help himself. The fury that had welled up in him at the sudden and totally unexpected sight of Foss's hated face—it had simply overwhelmed him. That combined with Foss's casual slaying of Noah had been too much for Sutton.

He swung his sledge over his shoulder and brought it down to smash a boulder. He was barely aware of the two prisoners scooping up the pulverized quartz and pouring it into buckets. He was hardly conscious of the sun burning down upon his head and bent back or of the sweat that was squeezing from his skin.

The sledge in his hand became a weapon. He imagined

Foss's face leering up at him from the pitted surface of a slab of quartz. He slammed the hammer down on the slab, shattering it and sending shards of quartz flying through the air.

"Take it more slow," muttered a man on his left as he wiped the sweat from his forehead. "You'll be all wore out before the day's half done. And wore out here means you'll be gun-shot sure."

Sutton knew the man was right. But he couldn't seem to help himself. Fueled by his fury and stoked by his lust for vengeance, his body was a furnace that he knew might explode if he didn't vent his rage in hard work. He would not give in to that rage, not again, he vowed. One mistake was bad enough. He wouldn't allow himself to make a second one. He would wait and watch, bide his time, and, when a chance presented itself, he would strike. And Foss would die.

But he knew he had to be careful. He could kill Foss easily enough—he knew he had the means to kill the man at almost any time he chose. But he couldn't risk getting killed himself by the guards an instant after having accomplished his goal. Getting killed was unthinkable to him because it would mean, not just his own death, but that Johnny Loud Thunder would escape his vengeance.

The urge to act—specifically, to kill Foss—was strong within Sutton. As he brought the sledge up over his shoulder, he caught sight of Foss, who was standing not far away with Thorne and pointing at him. He kept his feet planted firmly where they were and brought the sledge down, sweat dripping from his face as he did so.

A moment later Thorne came up to him and said, "Sutton, you're through here for now."

Was this it then? Sutton wondered. Had Foss ordered Thorne to kill him here and now? His hands tightened on the handle of the sledge hammer.

"You're going down into the mine," Thorne told him. "I guess Carew wanted to do you a favor. Get you out of this hot sun before you roast in your own sweat. Come on."

Sutton let go of the sledge hammer and it fell to the ground. He walked around the boulders and headed toward the ridge in the distance. "I could use a drink of water," he said to Thorne as he walked.

"Barrel's over there," Thorne said, pointing to where it stood under the hot sun.

Sutton turned and went over to it. He was filling the tin dipper with tepid water when he heard Foss call Thorne's name.

As he raised the dipper to his lips, Thorne knocked it from his hand. Sutton looked down at the dipper and then at Thorne.

Thorne said, "You must have made Carew mad same as you did Kirby yesterday. He just told me that you're not to have any water."

Sutton headed for the ridge, Thorne right behind him, a Colt in his hand.

When they rounded it, Sutton saw the entrance to the mine for the first time since he had been captured. The tunnel had been hollowed out of the side of the ridge not far from Deep Creek. It sloped down into the earth and the men, like slow ants, entered and left it as Sutton walked toward it. Flanking the tunnel on both sides were tall mounds of tailings.

"Down we go," Thorne said when they reached the mine's entrance. "Grab hold of one of those pickaxes."

Sutton picked up one that leaned against the wheel of a wagon, thinking with muted pleasure that there were a lot of potential weapons lying around loose in the area. He fingered the sharp point on one end of the pickax in his hand as he made his way into the shaft. A pickax like this, he thought, could pierce a man's skull with no trouble at all.

Candles, with polished pieces of tin behind them to serve as reflectors, burned in niches in the tunnel's walls. Timbers propped up its roof in places. Here and there water dripped from the ceiling of the tunnel.

Sutton found himself breathing hard in the air, which was both foul and thick with dust. Stooped men, naked to the waist, passed him carrying broad-banded haversacks over their shoulders. Bent nearly double, they made their slow way up to the mouth of the shaft, the sound of their ragged breathing humming in the humid air.

"You're going to coyote," Thorne told Sutton as they made their way deeper into the earth.

"What's that?"

"Coyoting? That's digging side tunnels off the main one to get at the gold in the quartz that's resting on bedrock. Like that tunnel shooting off over there."

Sutton saw the tunnel Thorne had referred to, which branched off at right angles to the main one. It was shored up with stout posts and caps.

"You can start your coyoting right here," Thorne said.

"There's barely enough room to stand up straight down here," Sutton said, "let alone room enough to swing a pickax."

"Only way to do it is to get down on your knees," Thorne said.

Sutton stared at Thorne, at the smile on the man's face.

Thorne hefted the Colt in his hand. "Get down and get going, Sutton. You're wasting time."

Sutton got down on his knees, his eyes still on Thorne's face.

Thorne stood smiling in front of him, his legs spread, his eyes gleaming in the candlelight. "You look to me like a man unaccustomed to being on his knees, Sutton," he commented. "But you'll get used to it. Maybe not even mind it after a bit. In fact, you might even get to like it since you'll learn that I don't give a man I've got on his knees too much trouble.

"We've had come cocky hombres like you working here before, Sutton. They all cracked. Some sooner, some later. But crack they all did. I guess there's something just naturally humbling about having to spend so much of your life on your knees like you have to do down here. It seems to kind of crush a man's spirit—makes him real docile after a time." Thorne's smile vanished. "Speaking of docile, Sutton, it's high time you started calling me Mr. Thorne. You got that?"

"I got it."

"You don't! I just told you to call me . . ."

"Mr. Thorne," Sutton said evenly, his eyes still on Thorne's face.

"Now there you go! That's better." Thorne's smile returned. "Now get to work." He crouched down some distance from Sutton, nodded to a guard with a drawn gun who was making his way down the shaft, and began to roll a cigarette after holstering his revolver.

Sutton swung the pickax against the side of the tunnel and dislodged dirt which fell between his knees and the tunnel's wall. His second swing struck bedrock.

"Work up above that bedrock," Thorne ordered.

Sutton did and was soon up to his thighs in loose dirt. Although the work wasn't hard, he sweated in the warm and fetid air of the shaft. The sweat dripped from his face as he swung the pickax over and over again. Then, dropping it, he stripped off his shirt and dropped it behind him to prevent it from being buried in the dirt he was dislodging as he worked.

Around him, shadows cast by the dancing candle flames darted and leaped. Behind him, Thorne whistled softly.

"How long you figure you'll last at this?" Thorne suddenly asked.

"Long as I have to," Sutton answered. "Longer maybe."

Thorne's boot caught him in the small of the back. He started to rise but Thorne was standing over him, his Colt again in his hand.

"How many *times* have I got to tell you?" Thorne asked angrily.

"I'll be sure to remember next time, *Mister* Thorne." Sutton turned back to his work.

He worked in a world of less than half-light, a world outside of time. Sutton's was a world of aching muscles and sore knees, of eyes stinging from the salty sweat that ran into them, of seemingly endless labor.

Thorne shouted a summons at one point and someone came to kneel beside Sutton. The man scooped up some of the dirt surrounding Sutton and placed it in a haversack which, when it was full, he carried away. He returned and

LUKE SUTTON: INDIAN FIGHTER

repeated the process. Sutton's pickax struck the dirt wall again and again and he began to move into the hollow he had made, crawling along it slowly, deepening it, sneezing as the dirt clogged his nostrils, coughing as it worked its way from his nose down into his throat.

He desperately wanted water. But he wouldn't let himself ask Thorne for it. Thorne, he was certain, would welcome the chance to refuse his request.

In the not-day and not-night world of the tunnel he was coyoting, Sutton deliberately thought of rare and bloody beefsteaks, of tart wine, of boiled yams buried in freshly churned butter. His efforts were futile; no saliva filled his mouth. It remained dry as the dust that was floating in the air around him.

He had no idea how many hours had passed when he heard Thorne call his name from the main shaft.

"You ready to consider quitting for the day?" Thorne called to him.

"I'll consider it," Sutton called back cautiously, not sure whether Thorne was taunting him or not. And then, remembering, he added, "Mr. Thorne."

Thorne's laughter echoed behind Sutton. "Come on! Crawl on out of there, coyote!"

Sutton, his pickax in his hand, crawled backward on his hands and knees and then dropped down from the bedrock to stand, slightly stooped, on the floor of the main shaft before Thorne.

"Let's go," Thorne said. "You first."

Sutton looked around for his shirt. It wasn't where he had left it. He finally found it on the far side of the shaft, directly behind Thorne. He picked it up, put it on, and started up the steeply sloping shaft with Thorne following close behind him.

When he came out of the mine, he stood blinking in the light that blinded him despite the fact that the sun was down. He rubbed his eyes with his fists, tried to spit to clear the dirt from his mouth but found he couldn't because his mouth was too dry, and then he just stood there squinting at the blurred outlines of trees and men in the distance.

The men were formed into the familiar double column and, as other men left the mine, they fell into it.

Before Thorne could order him to do so, Sutton walked over and got in line behind the last man in the column. Minutes later, a guard barked an order and the men began to move around the ridge toward the stockade.

On the way to it, Sutton remembered that he had left his hat inside the stockade. He wondered how he would manage to eat if it had been stolen and if the wagon bed contained the same gruel this night as it had the night before. He remembered something Noah had said.

Fingers were invented before forks.

So he'd get by, he told himself.

"Halt!"

Sutton glanced at Thorne, who had shouted the order as the double column abruptly halted in response to it. Thorne was talking to another guard and both of them were staring at him.

Sutton looked away.

And then Thorne and the guard were standing next to him.

"This here the man you mean?" Thorne asked the guard.

"He's the one. I saw him just as plain."

Thorne reached out and dug his fingers into Sutton's shirt pocket. When his fingers emerged, they held a small piece of tightly folded paper. Thorne carefully unfolded it.

"See!" declared the guard triumphantly. "Didn't I tell you?"

Sutton's eyes narrowed as he watched Thorne's face.

Thorne was looking down at the paper in his hands. When he looked up at Sutton, he asked, "Now just what did you plan on doing with this? We got no general store here."

"Maybe he was going to try to bribe one of us," the guard suggested. "To look the other way and let him make a run for it."

"Get Carew!" Thorne told the guard. To Sutton, as he unholstered his Colt and aimed it at him, he said, "Fall out, coyote."

Sutton stepped out of the line and Thorne nodded to another guard, who moved the prisoners on toward the stockade.

Sutton remained silent, glancing at the paper that Thorne had refolded and was now holding in his free hand.

When Foss appeared, Thorne ordered the guard to hold his gun on Sutton.

Foss and Thorne talked in low tones for several minutes and then Sutton heard Foss swear vehemently. His epithet was quickly followed by angry words addressed to Thorne which Sutton couldn't hear.

Thorne, after turning over the folded piece of paper to Foss, turned back to Sutton. He motioned the guard away. Then he stepped back from Sutton, cocking his Colt.

"Somebody," Sutton said quietly, "ought to tell me why I'm about to be gunned down."

"For stealing gold!" Foss yelped eagerly.

"I stole no gold," Sutton said.

"I've got proof right here in my pocket that you did!" Foss said.

"The guard saw you steal it!" Thorne declared.

"That guard," Sutton said, "must have awful good eyes." He turned his head slightly, trying to judge whether he could make a run for the ridge. "There I was way inside that tunnel I was coyoting and—where was the guard? I don't recall him peeping over my shoulder while I worked."

"Shoot him, Thorne!" Foss ordered.

"Thorne," Sutton said quickly, "you planted that paper packet of gold dust in my shirt pocket while I was coyoting and I think I know why. This man in front of me—the one you call Carew—wants me dead. I think he had that guard set me up so's he'd have an excuse to kill me."

Frowning, Thorne said, "His name's Carew."

"His name's Adam Foss," Sutton countered. "Or was. But names don't matter. What matters is . . ."

Just before Thorne fired, Sutton dodged, threw himself on the ground, rolled as Thorne fired again, and then he was up and running.

He dodged from side to side as he ran toward the ridge, the sound of bullets whining in the air about him. He had almost reached the ridge when a guard rounded it and, when he spotted Sutton approaching, pulled his revolver and yelled, "Stop!"

Sutton had no choice. He skidded to a halt.

"Shoot him!" Foss screamed to the guard facing Sutton.

"He's a thief!" Thorne yelled at the top of his voice.

And then Sutton heard another voice bellow behind him.

"What the hell's going on here!" the voice roared.

Sutton recognized the voice as belonging to Kirby. He heard an angry conversation taking place behind him but he didn't turn around, remaining instead facing the guard with the drawn gun.

Moments later Kirby, Foss, and Thorne came up to stand in front of him.

"Look at him!" Kirby snarled, pointing at Sutton. "Strong as a brace of oxen! He's got staying power, this one has. He'll last a long time. And you were going to shoot him down, Thorne! Now where's there any sense in that?"

"But he stole some of our gold, Kirby," Foss protested. He pulled the piece of paper from his pocket and handed it to Kirby.

"I don't give a damn about this dust you were telling me about," Kirby declared, pocketing the paper.

"I don't see why you give a damn about *him!*" Foss shouted, jerking a thumb in Sutton's direction.

"Because, Carew," Kirby shouted back, "he'll last as long as a *year*, that's why!"

"But, Kirby, you can't just let him get away with what he did!" Foss argued. "He's got to pay! We can find lots of other men as tough as him. They're all over the Hills. Let me shoot him, Kirby."

"Shut up!" Kirby told Foss, holding up a hand in warning. "I run this outfit. My word's gospel around here. And I say you're not going to shoot him."

"But, Kirby . . ."

"Not one more word!" Kirby said ominously. "Not *one!*" His stern expression gradually softened as Foss remained silent. "I can understand you wanting to learn him a lesson. A commendable attitude indeed. So why don't you just turn him over to Thorne here for some of his special kind of schooling? The kind he metes out to contrary prisoners from time to time. Now how does that strike you?"

As Foss muttered his unenthusiastic agreement, Thorne said to the guard, "Let's take him over to my classroom."

As Kirby threw an arm around Foss's shoulder, Thorne and the guard marched Sutton to the south side of the stockade.

Sutton found himself facing two tall posts that had been notched at their tops. Across them had been laid a third post that rested in the notches. Looped over it were two long lengths of rope.

"Get another man," Thorne told the guard. "We'll need some help."

When the guard returned with a companion, Thorne pointed at Sutton and said, "Bare his back!"

When one of the guards had stripped Sutton's shirt from him and thrown it to the ground, Thorne barked, "Now hang him high!"

While one guard held his gun on Sutton, the other began to tie an end of one of the two ropes to his left wrist.

But, before he could finish the job, Sutton drew back his right arm and landed his fist on the guard's jaw. As the man staggered backward, Sutton made a grab for him, intending to use him as a shield against the gun in the hand of the other guard as well as the one Thorne was holding on him.

The man fell before Sutton could seize him and Thorne grabbed Sutton, spun him around, and landed a dizzying uppercut on his jaw.

"Get up!" he yelled at the guard lying groggily on the ground. "Get your gun back on him. I'll tie him myself." He began to fasten the rope to Sutton's left wrist as the two guards stood by, the barrels of their revolvers almost touching Sutton's body.

Thorne viciously knotted the rope around Sutton's wrist and then went to work on the other wrist. When he had bound both wrists, he stepped back and gave an order to the guards, who holstered their guns once Thorne had drawn his and aimed it at Sutton.

Each guard took one of the free ends of the two ropes that were looped over the ridgepole and then, pulling on them, hauled Sutton up until the toes of his boots barely touched the ground.

Thorne holstered his gun and said, "I'll be right back."

Sutton watched him enter his tent and emerge from it a moment later carrying a tightly woven rawhide bullwhip.

Thorne took up a position directly in front of Sutton and almost languidly cracked the whip. "I told you when we were down in the mine," he said, "that we had ways of breaking men like you. This here happens to be one of them." He snapped the whip again, not quite touching Sutton with it.

One of the guards holding the end of one of the ropes, his heels dug into the ground to brace himself, smiled.

Thorne walked around behind Sutton and then asked, "What's my name?"

"Thorne," Sutton answered.

Thorne's bullwhip *thwacked* against Sutton's bare back and his body jerked, the ropes biting into his wrists as he did so.

"What's my name?" Thorne asked again.

"Thorne," Sutton replied, rejecting the impulse to tense his muscles, knowing that if he did the whip would draw blood that much sooner.

The whip struck, coiling about Sutton's body like a leather snake. Sutton took the blow in grim silence, his fingers gripping the ropes tied to his wrists as he struggled in vain to gain a foothold on the ground.

"*Mister* Thorne!" Thorne yelled, and sent his whip slashing through the air.

Sutton's breath shot from his lungs as the whip hit him.

Thorne didn't speak again. Only his whip did each time it landed on Sutton's back with a sickening *thwack*.

Blood began to trickle down Sutton's back where Thorne's whip had sundered his skin.

"*Mister* Thorne," he heard Thorne mutter to himself. "You'll call me Mr. Thorne or I'll slice you up into sausage!"

Sutton's head dropped forward and, as Thorne's whip once again viciously embraced his body, he saw that the leather was now bright red with his own blood.

The whip withdrew, returned, withdrew.

And then the world around Sutton blurred. He shook his head to clear it but, as the whip once more cruelly circled his bleeding torso, he lost consciousness and plunged down into a black but mercifully whipless world.

Pain, the rider. Sutton, its mount.

He tried to unseat the pain, buck it away into the drifting darkness, but it would not be thrown. It tightened its dark grip on him and he cried out.

His return to consciousness was abrupt. But at first he thought he was still lost in that black world that was not a real world. The pain still rode him hard. He raised his head slowly. Fireflies punctured the night's darkness. The lanterns on the guards' perches looked like larger fireflies. The stars in the sky above were more distant fireflies burning with a white light.

Sutton found himself kneeling on the ground between the two upright poles to which the ropes that still bound his wrists had been tied. His arms were stretched out at right angles to his body. He fought his way to his feet and stood there thinking. Then, tentatively, he gripped the rope that bound his right wrist with his fingers and pulled on it. Nothing happened. He pulled harder. Still nothing happened. Digging his boots into the ground beneath him, he pulled again on the rope as hard as he could. The right post gave slightly, its top angling down toward him. He pulled again, his body straining, his mind focused on only one thing—freedom. His boot heels dug into the ground and his body leaning to the left, he continued to pull on the rope. The top of the pole on his right continued to tilt toward him, the ridgepole resting in its notch pointing at the sky.

He released his hold on the rope and it went slack, looping down toward but not touching the ground. Breathing hard, he sat down on the ground and twisted his body so that it faced the tilted pole on his right. He stretched out his right leg as far as it would go and then, pulling hard with his left hand on the rope that bound his left wrist, he raised his right leg while at the same time lowering his right hand.

Exultation raced through him as his fingers touched his right boot. He raised his leg higher and his fingers slid into his boot. When they emerged from it, they held his sheathed hunting knife. Deftly, he eased the knife from its sheath and began to saw on the rope binding his right wrist. When the rope gave way, he leaped to his feet and quickly cut through the rope that bound his left wrist. Then, with a glance at the nearest guard's perch, he stuffed the knife's sheath back into his boot and began to make his way toward Thorne's tent, the severed ends of the ropes dangling from his wrists.

When he reached the tent, he halted, listening. No sound came from within the tent. Carefully, he folded back the flap and stepped inside the tent where he stood still, listening carefully.

The sound of someone's soft breathing almost brought a smile to Sutton's face. He moved cautiously toward the sound, reached down with his free hand, and felt a body. "Thorne!" he muttered.

The body beneath his hand lurched. "Who . . ."

Sutton's left hand found Thorne's throat and his fingers circled it. "I've got a knife in my other hand, Thorne. It can do even worse things to you than your whip did to me."

"*Sutton!* How'd you . . ."

"I want what you took from me out on the trail, Thorne."

"The money—I've only got half of it. Markham's got the other half."

"I don't give a damn about the money. What I want is my .44—my rifle, all my gear."

"Let me up then and I'll get them."

Sutton released his grip on Thorne's throat and stepped back.

Thorne sat up. "I'll light a lamp," he said as he got to his feet.

"No light."

Thorne, in the moonlight entering the tent, rummaged about and then handed Sutton his cartridge belt from which his holstered Smith and Wesson hung.

Sutton took it and said, "You move, I'll throw this knife."

He quickly strapped his gun belt around his hips and then reached for the rifle Thorne was holding out to him. "Now get my saddle and the rest of my gear and then you're taking me to Foss—the man you call Carew."

Thorne chuckled. "Can't do that."

"What do you mean you can't?"

"He's gone."

"Gone?" Sutton felt a sense of bleak despair sweep over him as Thorne said, "He told Kirby he was clearing out. He collected his share of our gold and left not long after sundown last night. He didn't give a reason. He just up and went."

"I'm the reason he went," Sutton said. "Where'd he go?"

"He didn't tell Kirby—anybody, far as I know—where he was headed."

"Get my saddle and the rest of my gear," Sutton said. "We're getting out of here and going over to the corral." When Thorne had gathered up Sutton's gear, Sutton said, "You carry the gear. Now let's go."

He let Thorne, who was wearing only longjohns, precede him out of the tent and, as Sutton ducked out after him, he looked around quickly. There was no one in sight except the stockade's guards, most of whom were dozing on their perches in the weak light of their lanterns.

As Sutton and Thorne were passing the place where Thorne had whipped Sutton, Sutton said, "Hold it, Thorne. Pick up my shirt and stuff it in my saddlebag."

Thorne did as he was told and they moved on.

When they reached the corral, Sutton ordered Thorne to enter it and saddle his sorrel. He followed him into the corral and stood beside him as Thorne got the sorrel ready to ride.

When he had finished doing so, Sutton rammed his Winchester into the boot and got a grip on the reins. "Move out ahead of me, Thorne. Open that gate."

As Thorne swung the corral gate open, Sutton moved past him, leading his mount. Outside the corral, he brought the horse to a halt and stirruped a boot.

But before he could swing into the saddle, Thorne closed the corral gate and shouted, "*Guard!*"

Sutton stepped swiftly away from the sorrel and threw the knife that was still in his hand.

Thorne gasped as the knife struck him and bent over, his hands clutching its hilt, which protruded from his body on the left side of his rib cage.

"Who's out there?" a guard manning the nearest perch called, raising his lantern high above his head and peering out into the darkness.

Thorne sank to his knees. Before he could fall, Sutton stepped up to him and pulled the knife from his body. He wiped it on his jeans, shoved it into his boot, and then swung into the saddle. He glanced down once at Thorne's lifeless body lying sprawled below him on the ground and then galloped away into the night.

CHAPTER 9

Sutton rode shirtless and hatless through what remained of the night, heading northwest. He had pushed thoughts of Foss from his mind. There had been no way to pick up the man's trail in the darkness. No way to tell where he might be headed. There was no use, he had told himself, in wasting time trying to find Foss. He had no idea where he had gone or where he was at the moment. But he believed he did know where Johnny Loud Thunder was. If Linden's newspaper was correct, Johnny was scouting for Custer's Seventh Cavalry in Montana Territory.

When dawn came, Sutton reined in his sorrel and dismounted. He would sleep through most of the day—if his lacerated body would let him, he thought wryly.

He untied the severed ropes which still dangled from his wrists and threw them to the ground. Then he untied his bedroll, spread it on the ground beneath a hemlock and, after putting on his shirt, lay down upon it gingerly, his unholstered revolver at his side.

The sun was down when he awoke.

He got up and returned his bedroll to its place behind his saddle. The blood on his back had dried and formed ugly scabbed ridges, dark testaments to the flogging Thorne had given him.

Stroking his thickly stubbled chin as he rode along, he thought about Johnny Loud Thunder. Somewhere just beyond the horizon up there, he thought, is where I'll find him. Where I'll kill him.

The next day Sutton paused beside a creek only long enough to wash and dry his clothes and himself.

Two more days came and went as he rode relentlessly over mountains and on through the bunch grass that covered the plains, subsisting on small game—squirrels and, once, a skunk—he brought down.

When the Big Horn Mountains loomed on his left, he forded the Powder River and, the next day, the Tongue River. The following day, as he rode through the valley of the Little Big Horn River just after noon, he spotted the troops of the Seventh Cavalry passing over a divide in the distance and riding down into the valley at a fast trot.

They were moving in the standard four-abreast formation, their square regimental flag and smaller guidons flapping in the light breeze sweeping through the valley. Pack mules followed them under the guidance of a packmaster and behind the mules came light ambulance wagons.

Sutton immediately recognized the soldier leading the campaign-hatted troopers from descriptions he had read of the renowned Lieutenant Colonel George Armstrong Custer.

Custer was riding a sorrel gelding that was darker in color than Sutton's mount. He was wearing a blue flannel shirt, buckskin trousers tucked into long, highly polished boots, a broad-brimmed white hat, and a brace of pistols. Custer's long yellow hair was neatly trimmed as was his thick mustache. As Sutton rode closer to him, he was able to make out Custer's piercing blue eyes.

He turned his horse and headed for Custer but, before he reached him, someone barked an order and a sergeant, accompanied by four troopers, rode out and cut him off.

The sergeant held up a hand and the troopers behind him halted. "State your business," he said to Sutton.

"Want a word with Custer."

"What about?"

"I didn't say I wanted a word with you, Sergeant."

The sergeant hesitated a moment and then gestured.

The troopers behind him moved forward to flank Sutton, two on each side of him. Then, turning his horse, the sergeant rode back toward the column, Sutton and the troopers following him.

When they had rejoined the column, the sergeant spoke to Custer. "Sir, this man says he wants to have a talk with you."

Custer shot an appraising glance at Sutton. And then he nodded curtly to the sergeant, who drew back with the four troopers.

"Afternoon, General," Sutton said, using the man's wartime brevet rank. "I read about how you were coming out here to Montana Territory to chase Indians. So I came looking for you." He fell in and rode along beside Custer.

Custer glanced at Sutton. "You have a desire to enlist in the cavalry then, I take it, Mr. . . . ."

"Luke Sutton, General. No, enlisting is one thing I don't happen to have in mind. I spent enough time with the army some years back as a scout."

"You said you came looking for me," Custer said stiffly. "So I thought . . ."

"I thought I might be of some help to you, General," Sutton said offhandedly.

"In what way, Mr. Sutton?"

"Well, take a look off there to the right. See those ashes blowing in the wind? Indians camped over there not long ago. If it had been long ago those ashes would have blown away by now. Those horse droppings up ahead—they're moist, almost fresh enough to still steam."

"We know there are Indians ahead of us, Mr. Sutton," Custer snapped. "We are on our way to attack them before they can elude us."

"How many do you figure on attacking, General?"

"Several hundred perhaps."

"Could be more like thousands," Sutton said, "judging by the width of the trail they left."

Custer turned to an officer riding just behind him and asked, "Is Bloody Knife still out scouting, Major Reno?"

"No, sir," Reno replied. "He came back some time ago and is riding farther back. With the pack train, I believe."

"Send someone to tell him to ride up here," Custer said, and Reno relayed the order to a sergeant.

When the Arikara scout rode up on Sutton's left some minutes later, Custer leaned forward in his saddle and, speaking around Sutton to Bloody Knife, said, "This man—Mr. Sutton thinks more than a few hundred Indians have recently passed this way. Bloody Knife, I believe that is your opinion as well, is it not?"

Bloody Knife, an elderly man who was wearing a shirt, trousers, and a bright red strip of flannel to hold his long gray hair in place, didn't answer the question immediately.

When he did, he said simply, "I have told you, my friend, that there are more Sioux and Cheyenne ahead of us than there are bullets in the belts of all your soldiers."

"The lay of the land ahead of us," Sutton said, "tells the tale. It looks like a cattle drive just passed through here."

Bloody Knife said, "There may be as many as one thousand warriors."

"I'll raise you," Sutton said to him. "More like two thousand or I miss my bet."

"And we're trotting!" Custer exclaimed somewhat peevishly. "We should be *galloping!* If those Indians escape us—that would be a most humiliating defeat, to say the very least."

Before Custer could give the order to speed up the column's advance, Bloody Knife said to him, "Old friend, the troopers are tired—nearly exhausted. So are their horses. When I returned from scouting, they told me you marched them since ten o'clock last night and . . ."

"We halted at two o'clock!" Custer interrupted angrily.

"But at eight o'clock this morning," said Major Reno from behind Custer, "you resumed the march."

"I will not let those Indians get away from me!" Custer practically shouted.

Bloody Knife grunted and said, "I have been told that another four men deserted last night."

"Ruffians!" Custer exploded. "Not soldiers. Soldiers—staunch soldiers—do not desert."

"The horses need water, sir," said Reno in a mild voice. "That water back in the ravine where we camped was too alkaline for them to drink. The animals can't eat the oats the men have tried to feed them. The grain is too dry and the horses are too parched. The oats just drop from their mouths."

"They'll have water," Custer said sharply, "when we reach Ash Creek."

"General," Sutton said, "how many men do you have with you?"

"Six hundred."

Sutton's low whistle blended with the clinking of tin mess cups and the jingling of harnesses behind him.

"How do you think you can be of help to me, Mr. Sutton?" Custer inquired.

"You can never have too many scouts," Sutton answered. "And I'm an experienced scout. I had an Apache for a teacher and a real fine teacher that man was, too. Learned lots from him. I'd like to scout for you, General."

"The army pays its scouts only . . ."

Sutton held up a hand. "I'm not interested in the pay, General."

Custer gave Sutton a puzzled glance. "Just what is it you *are* interested in, Mr. Sutton?"

"One of your scouts. One who calls himself Johnny Loud Thunder."

Bloody Knife grunted and Sutton glanced at him. "Do you know Johnny, Bloody Knife?" he asked.

"Part Cheyenne," Bloody Knife answered. "Part wolf."

"Where might I be liable to find him?" Sutton asked, careful to keep the excitement he was feeling out of his voice.

Bloody Knife pointed.

"South," Sutton said softly to himself. "Well, General, if it's agreeable to you, suppose I head south and see what I can find out for you."

"Go right ahead, Mr. Sutton," Custer said. "Bloody Knife

can brief you concerning his most recent findings before you go. But I have a question. What is the nature of your interest in Loud Thunder?"

"Met him down in Texas one time and haven't seen him since," Sutton answered evasively, and then rode away with Bloody Knife.

When Bloody Knife halted his horse some distance from the column, Sutton waited for him to speak. Almost a minute passed during which Sutton slapped at some buffalo gnats as tiny as dust particles that were circling his head to prevent them from stinging him.

Finally Bloody Knife spoke. "He is my good friend," he said, sitting his saddle and watching Custer ride off at the head of the cavalry column. "In the war that divided your people and set them to fighting with one another, he was a brave soldier." Bloody Knife fell silent for a moment and then continued speaking. "There have been bad omens. There was a snowstorm three weeks ago when we were camped at the Yellowstone River and yet it is summer now. I think my friend will die in the battle that is about to be, as I will."

"Then you think I cut the sign left by those Indians right?" Sutton asked.

Bloody Knife nodded. "You cut the sign correctly. Up on the Yellowstone," he added, "all the scouts—Crow as well as Arikara—we all rode in a great circle and sang our death songs. We have since held ceremonies to seek the protection of the spirits. They have not answered us. I will die. So will Yellow Hair. I grieve for him."

"From what I've seen so far," Sutton said somberly,

"things don't look the best, that's for certain. Well, I'll scout south of here."

"You know what to look for?" Bloody Knife asked.

"Dead fires and whether they're cold or warm. The position of lodge pole pins to see how big the lodges were and how many warriors they sheltered. That sort of thing."

"The Apache you spoke of to Yellow Hair, he taught you well, as you claimed." Bloody Knife looked up at the sun and made the sign for farewell. Still gazing at the sun, he said solemnly, "I shall not see you go down behind the hills tonight." Then he rode back to rejoin the passing cavalry column.

Sutton spurred his sorrel and soon left the Seventh far behind him as he galloped south. He rode in the lee of a bluff for some time, barely aware of the bright color of wild rosebushes in vivid bloom all around him. The ground beneath him, he noticed, was cut almost to powder that was six inches deep by lodgepoles that had been dragged by Indian ponies. Little grass remained on it and he realized that the Indians ahead of him must have an enormous number of ponies to leave the terrain clipped almost completely clean of grass. Alkaline dust rose up around him as he rode on, causing him to cough.

Next to no grass, he thought. He hoped Custer's mules were packing enough grain for themselves and the horses since they'd find no other forage.

He traveled on and then stopped when he came upon a huge camp circle where lodgepoles still stood in place.

Sun dance, he thought. That's what they did here. Which means they're in no hurry. Custer needn't worry about losing track of these Indians or of them getting away from him, he thought. More likely, he'll catch up to them and when he does there's going to be hell to pay.

He dismounted and examined the ground around him. He hunkered down and felt the ashes of a fire. Cool but not cold. He counted the remains of more than forty fires around him. He got up and examined the positions of the lodgepole pins, concluding that each of the lodges that had stood where he was now standing had been large ones. Near another dead fire he noticed a pile of gnawed buffalo ribs. He picked one up and found it had not yet dried out.

Getting back into the saddle, he rode on for several miles, scanning the countryside for any sign of Johnny Loud Thunder. He found none.

When he reached a bluff on the northern bank of the Little Big Horn, he rode up it and dismounted just before reaching its top. He left his horse, reins trailing on the ground, and, careful not to skyline himself, made his way up to the top of the bluff where he dropped down on the ground and looked out over the plain on the far side of the river.

The Indians were camped there, he found, and their lodges, he noted, were almost countless. There must be hundreds of them, he thought, scattered about the immense campsite. And on the edge of the encampment ponies grazed by the thousands.

Sutton nodded grimly. He'd been right. Bloody Knife had been right. Six hundred men Custer's got, he thought, and he's worried about all these Indians getting away from him. He shook his head, having seen enough.

He made his way back down the bluff to his horse, got into the saddle, and rode north at a swift gallop.

He found the Seventh in midafternoon near the headwaters of Ash Creek. Horses were drinking the clear creek water. Men lay sprawled on the ground. Troopers, with their horses' reins wrapped around their arms, lay sleeping perilously close to their horses' front feet. A horse whinnied as a trooper applied salve to its back where sweat beneath its saddle had opened bloody sores.

Sutton rode through the bivouac, noticing the haggard expressions on the troopers' faces and noticing too that more than one man had his eyelids swollen almost shut as a result of buffalo gnat stings.

Six hundred worn-out men, he thought as he searched for Custer. He passed a trooper who was cursing as he examined the blisters that had formed on the inside of his thighs, the result, Sutton knew, of having ridden too long and too hard. He recalled Major Reno's remark about Custer having stopped his men at two o'clock in the morning and then marched them on again a mere six hours later. He thought of the countless Sioux and Cheyenne he had come upon.

He found Custer by the bank of the creek, arms folded over his chest, face placid. "Sir," he said.

Custer looked up at him.

Sutton told him what he had discovered. "Those Indians aren't more than ten to fifteen miles from here and they don't show any sign of being in a hurry to go anywhere."

"They undoubtedly don't know we're after them," Custer said, smiling.

"Those mules of yours," Sutton said.

"Mules, Mr. Sutton?"

"Don't they ever stop braying?"

Custer seemed to become aware of the harsh braying of the mules only at that moment.

"I wouldn't be a bit surprised," Sutton said, "if the Indians —especially if they've got scouts out—know you're here, thanks to those mules.

"By the way, General, I didn't see any sign of Johnny Loud Thunder. He's come back here?"

"I haven't seen him."

"Well, I'll just have myself a look around. Maybe I'll be lucky enough to run"—Sutton had been about to say "run him down" but said instead—"run into him." He turned his horse and picked his way among troopers, ambulance wagons, and pack mules. He didn't find Johnny Loud Thunder. He did find Bloody Knife, who was sitting morosely on the ground, his back resting against the wheel of an ambulance wagon.

"Did Johnny Loud Thunder come back from his scouting expedition?" Sutton asked the scout.

"He will not come back."

Sutton stiffened. "He's dead?"

"He is alive," Bloody Knife said. "Mitch Bouyer just returned from scouting north of the river. He saw Loud Thunder riding with a party of Sioux led by Chief Gall."

"Then he's gone over to the Indians' side!" Sutton exclaimed excitedly, glad that the breed was still alive, glad that he still had a chance to wreak his long-delayed vengeance on the man.

"What did you find?" Bloody Knife asked Sutton, looking up at him for the first time since he had arrived beside the scout.

Sutton told him.

"Bouyer saw what you saw."

"Has he told Custer?"

"He has gone to do so," Bloody Knife said, and added, "It will be a big fight."

Sutton nodded and wheeled his horse. As he started back the way he had come, he heard the bugler sound Officers' Call. At the same moment he saw Major Reno and another officer, a captain, making their way on foot to where Custer still stood on the bank of the creek, his bugler beside him.

Sutton touched his spurs to the flanks of his sorrel and moved toward Custer, taking up a position some distance from the bank of the creek but close enough to hear what Custer was telling his officers.

"You, Captain Benteen," Custer was saying, "will take three companies and sweep the bluffs south of the river valley. I don't want any Indians you find left alive.

"Major Reno, you will also take three companies and go down Ash Creek, ford the Little Big Horn, and charge upon the southern end of the Indian encampment. I'll have five companies with me and will support you."

Sutton stared at Custer in disbelief, wondering how the man dared split his relatively small force into three separate units, wondering what possible military motive the man might have in doing so. Then, recalling what he had read about Custer's daring—some said too daring—tactics, which he had employed during the Civil War, he decided that Custer was employing the same kind of tactics here on the plains. If those tactics worked, he thought, Custer would probably prevail. If they didn't . . .

Sutton dismissed the thought from his mind and listened as Custer assigned another company and small details to be taken from each of the other companies to guard the slow-moving pack train.

Sutton's disbelief grew with every word Custer spoke. He was willing to concede that the pack train and the supplies and ammunition it carried were important but he was not willing to concede that it required so many soldiers to guard it—troopers taken from what he considered to be, even at full strength, a force that was far too small relative to the superior strength of the Sioux and Cheyenne.

Custer dismissed his officers and, as he walked away from the creek, Sutton rode up to him. "General, is it all right with you if I ride along with Major Reno and his men?"

"There will be heavy fighting," Custer cautioned him.

"I expect so," Sutton said, thinking of Johnny Loud Thunder.

"Well," Custer said, "try not to make a nuisance of yourself, Mr. Sutton."

"I'll try hard not to do that, General. Good luck to you."

Custer nodded and walked away.

Sutton turned his head and watched Reno's non-commissioned officers rouse the men of the three companies Custer had assigned to the major.

Then, as the bugler sounded General Call, all the troopers began to get themselves, their mounts, and their equipment ready to move out. While they were doing so, Sutton watered his sorrel at the creek, after which he obtained oats for it and a campaign hat for himself from the packmaster. He unsaddled the animal, shook out his saddle blanket, refolded it, and then put it and his gear back on his horse.

The bugler sounded Boots and Saddles and, as Sutton swung into the saddle, Captain Benteen moved out with his men, heading south to search for Indians on the bluffs south of the river.

As Major Reno led his men along the southern bank of Ash Creek, Sutton sat his horse. When the last trooper had ridden past him, he moved out and rode well out on the rear of the column's left flank as it moved toward the south fork of the Little Big Horn River.

"Who might you be?" a middle-aged trooper, obviously a veteran, asked him.

"A scout," Sutton responded.

"See any Indians, scout?" a young recruit asked.

"Not at the moment," Sutton replied. "But I expect we'll be seeing two or three by and by."

"It doesn't make sense to me," the veteran muttered, shaking his head. "Sending a man who's never fought Indians out to lead us right into their arms."

"You mean Major Reno?" Sutton asked the man.

"He's the one riding up there in the lead, ain't he?"

The recruit said, "Some men I've talked to say he had a good record in the war."

"He also got himself court-martialed, I heard," the veteran retorted. "For 'conduct unbecoming an officer and a gentleman.' The major has an eye for the ladies. And a taste for the bottle too, I'm told. One of the mule packers was telling me before we started out just now he'd seen Reno tippling from a bottle he took from his saddlebag and he said the major wasn't just checking to make sure it wasn't empty. The packer said he almost emptied all that was left in it."

"Making free with the ladies," the recruit mused, "don't seem to me to be a court-martial kind of offense. Besides, Custer himself's been court-martialed for more serious things than that. Like for disobeying orders and once for ordering one of his officers to shoot deserters if he could find them."

"Well, all that's in the past," the veteran trooper muttered. "What we got here in the present is Indians to fret about."

"I'm not worried," said the recruit.

"You ought to be," Sutton told him. "If you're not, you might get careless and it doesn't do a man a bit of good to get careless in a fracas with Indians."

He rode up the column's flank, noticing as he did so that Bloody Knife was riding on the right flank not far behind Reno. There were other scouts, ranging farther out on both flanks, both white men and Indians.

When they reached the bluffs, which were five to ten feet high in places along the Little Big Horn, the column moved along them, searching for a safe place to ford the river. When they finally found one, they paused briefly to let their horses submerge their muzzles in the cold water and then the crossing began.

The column broke badly during the ford and, as Sutton rode through the deep water, he noticed that Major Reno seemed to be having trouble handling his horse. But Reno finally reached the far bank and sat his horse while waiting for his troopers to re-form their four-abreast column.

Sutton had just come out of the river when he heard Reno give the order to attack the village that was visible in the distance.

Reno went galloping down the river valley toward the campsite, his troopers struggling to match the pace he had set.

Sutton galloped along with them, his .44 unholstered and held tightly in his right hand, an image of Johnny Loud Thunder bright in his mind.

Up ahead of Reno, he saw warriors, both on foot and mounted, come charging out of the Indian campsite and start toward the troopers, only to suddenly halt and begin wheeling in a circle, raising a great cloud of dust as they did so.

The Indians didn't appear to Sutton to be willing to close with the cavalry. In fact, as he galloped toward them, he saw them fall back toward their campsite.

Suspecting a trap, Sutton spurred his horse in order to catch up with Reno and tell him of his suspicion. But, before he reached him, Reno suddenly called a halt and ordered his men to dismount.

Sutton reined in his sorrel, wondering why Reno had given the command since there had been no engagement with the Indians.

Suddenly, a horse bolted and carried its trooper toward the Indians. The man was knocked from his horse by several warriors and shot. At the same time, Reno ordered every fourth man in each rank to take four horses and move them into a stand of timber that was off to the right near the river.

Sutton couldn't make out the next order Reno shouted but he saw the remaining soldiers—no more than eighty, he estimated—form a thin skirmish line, its right end anchored in the timber.

The troopers began firing their .45-caliber Springfield carbines and Army Colts at the Indians. Wildly, in too many cases, Sutton observed. Reno's made a bad mistake, he thought as he rode up behind the skirmish line and got off a shot at the Indians who were charging the troopers. He's gone from the offensive to a defensive position by ordering his men to dismount. He's lost the advantage mounted cavalry has and turned his troopers into just another batch of infantry soldiers. Sutton's next shot sent an Indian careening from his pony.

As the sound of carbines and Army Colts continued, the Indians swept around the end of Reno's line, turning his left flank. At almost the same moment warriors who had slipped upriver attacked the right flank, creating a deadly crossfire with their long-range Winchester repeaters.

"*Retreat!*" Reno shouted at the top of his voice. "Fall back into the woods!"

A soldier beside Sutton took a bullet in his chest and fell to the ground.

Sutton quickly got out of the saddle, lifted the wounded man, and threw him over his saddle. Then, ducking down and leading his sorrel, he raced through the continuing crossfire toward the woods.

CHAPTER 10

The skirmish line crumbled. Troopers ran past Sutton on their way to the woods. One of them dropped his carbine as a Sioux arrow embedded itself in his back.

A trooper running on Sutton's left suddenly swerved and raced toward Sutton, whom he pushed aside. He pulled the wounded man from Sutton's saddle and climbed clumsily up onto Sutton's horse.

Sutton, still holding his sorrel's reins, jerked them sharply and the sorrel pulled back. As it did, Sutton swung his right hand, which still held his .44, and clubbed the trooper from the saddle. He bent down to pick up the wounded man but, as he did so, an arrow struck the man in the neck.

Sutton recognized death when he saw it. Leading his horse, he ran on toward the timber and then in among the trees and the dense thorny rose- and plum-brush undergrowth beneath them. The light was less intense under the trees and it took Sutton several minutes to become fully accustomed to the shadowy world he found himself in, a world in which horses were screaming, carbines firing, men yelling and cursing, and Major Reno shouting orders that could not be heard above the terrible din.

Sutton took up a position just inside the timber behind the thickest tree trunk he could find. He pulled his Winchester

from the boot, holstering his revolver at the same time. He
wrapped the reins of his horse around his left wrist, dropped
to one knee, and brought his rifle up. His first shot downed a
Cheyenne who, along with the other warriors, had moved up
close to the timber during the cavalry's retreat. He was about
to fire a second shot when a riderless horse bolted past him,
knocking his rifle from his hands. To retrieve it, he realized,
he would have to expose himself to the Indians' fire.

A trooper behind him let out an agonized scream and fell
on top of Sutton. Sutton eased the wounded man to the
ground. The man's fingers were frantically clawing at the
arrow that protruded from his chest. Then they slowly
relaxed, went limp, and the trooper's eyes glazed. Sutton
picked up the man's dropped carbine. Behind and around
him men still swore, their voices shrill with fear and confu-
sion.

The recruit he had spoken to during the march dropped
down beside him. "I've never seen so many Indians in one
place at one time before!" he moaned. "What's that music I
hear?"

"War flutes," Sutton replied as the thin music blended eerily with the sound of gunfire. "Where's your carbine?" Sutton asked the recruit, squeezing off another shot that hit and
downed an Indian pony, sending its rider hurtling to the
ground.

"I don't know," the recruit answered. "I think I must've
dropped it when we ran."

"Use your Colt!" Sutton said sharply.

The recruit obediently drew his Army Colt and Sutton saw
his hand tremble as he fired it. Sutton continued firing until
his carbine suddenly fouled. Cursing, he examined the

weapon and found that it had become heated, causing the soft copper shell beneath the hammer to expand. The ejector had cut through the cartridge's rim, jamming it in place. He used his knife to work the cartridge out as bullets clipped the underbrush around him and arrows flew over his head.

"Where's Major Reno?" the recruit asked Sutton, looking around in the dimness beneath the trees.

"Keep your eyes on the Indians," Sutton told him. "They'll kill you. Reno won't."

Two horses ran out of the woods and, almost instantly, Indian arrows pierced their bodies. One horse fell. The other ran on only to fall beneath a blow from a war club that caught it just above the eyes.

"Oh, my *Lord!*" cried the recruit.

Sutton felt the man move and then stand up. "Get down!" he snapped, reaching up to pull the recruit down beside him.

The recruit eluded his grasp and murmured, "I've never been so scared before *ever!*"

Sutton grabbed the recruit's belt and pulled him down to the ground. "Use that gun you've got!" he commanded. But the recruit only shook his head, tears running down his cheeks.

Sutton smelled smoke.

A moment later he saw flames shoot up from the dry river-bottom grass and begin to spread into the buffalo-berry brush growing near it.

"They're trying to fry us!" a trooper yelled from behind Sutton. "They don't know how to fight fair!" he added at the top of his anguished voice.

Sutton almost smiled, thinking that the Indians might not know how to fight fair in cavalry terms but they sure did know how to fight if winning was their aim.

From behind the flames, the Indians launched arrows high into the air and, as they fell, many struck the backs of troopers lying flat on the ground as they fired at their attackers. Others struck horses which tore free of the men desperately trying to hold onto them and crashed out into the open to be brought down by the Indians.

"That is Crazy Horse," a voice said, and Sutton turned to find Bloody Knife, a carbine in his hands, kneeling where the recruit, who had disappeared, had been.

Bloody Knife pointed and Sutton saw the lone Indian crawling along the ground in front of the smoke, making his way toward the timber.

Crazy Horse suddenly leaped to his feet, raised his Winchester, and released a volley of shots. In the timber, a man cried out in pain.

"Chief Gall," said Bloody Knife, pointing to another Indian who had leaped out of the thick smoke and fired into the timber.

Where is Johnny Loud Thunder? Sutton asked himself as he aimed his carbine at Crazy Horse, fired, and missed the man.

Crazy Horse dropped down to the ground and, crawling backward, disappeared into the smoke. A moment later Chief Gall was swallowed up by it as well.

The flames of the fires the Indians had set shot along the ground and began to ignite the plum brush growing beneath the trees.

As the battle continued, a breeze sprang up and parted the gray curtain of smoke.

"They're retreating!" Sutton said to Bloody Knife. "They're heading back toward their camp."

Some of the Indians clearly were, led by Crazy Horse and Gall.

"Not retreating," Bloody Knife said. "They have some plan. Of that you can be sure."

Sutton decided that Bloody Knife was probably right. More than half the warriors remained after Gall and Crazy Horse had vanished, appearing and then disappearing again in the smoke like deadly apparitions.

Reno came crashing through the underbrush, his hat missing, his trousers tearing on the thorns of the rosebushes. "What do they intend?" he asked Bloody Knife, dropping down on one knee beside the scout.

"They may circle around behind us," Bloody Knife answered, and Sutton thought he detected a note of resignation in the man's voice.

"*The woods are burning!*" a trooper cried out, leaping to his feet and moving farther back into the timber.

"Can you see Custer?" Reno asked Bloody Knife.

The scout shook his head.

"Where *is* the man?" Reno roared. "He was to follow and back us up!"

Bloody Knife said, "Yellow Hair may have decided to attack the campsite at some other point."

Reno let out a vivid oath and stood up. "*To your horses!*" he shouted. "Move to the bluffs across the river!"

Almost every trooper immediately stopped firing. Many of them jumped up and began to search through the timber for their horses.

The Indians intensified their firing. Bullets and arrows tore into the trees.

Several troopers were looking around, obviously puzzled,

obviously unaware of Reno's shouted order, which had not reached them because of the intense noise.

"Are we getting out?" one of them called out to an officer who was struggling to quiet his rearing horse.

"To your horses, men!" the officer shouted in reply.

The remaining troopers leaped to their feet and scrambled through the underbrush, looking for their mounts.

"What damn fool move is this?" a trooper bellowed in a disgusted tone of voice.

No one answered him.

A group of Sioux suddenly emerged from the swirling smoke and fired a point-blank volley from less than thirty feet from the trees.

One of the bullets struck Bloody Knife, who had risen to his feet and was standing beside Reno. The bullet caught him between the eyes, shattering his skull and splattering Reno's face with blood.

As Bloody Knife fell beside Sutton, Reno seemed to succumb to panic. He ordered his men to dismount, apparently forgetting his original order to ford the river and take up a position on the bluffs on its far side.

Some of the men began to dismount. Others remained mounted, their horses rearing and circling under them.

Smoke drifted among the trees, mixing with blue gun smoke and bringing tears to the eyes of many of the troopers.

"Major," Sutton said to Reno, "we're outnumbered ten to one, looks like to me."

Reno didn't speak. He stood staring down at the faceless body of Bloody Knife lying at his feet, wiping the gore from his face.

"Major Reno," Sutton said more loudly, with a glance at

the Indians. "Your order to try to make the bluffs across the river—we'd best try to carry it out, seems to me. That high ground over there might give us a chance to . . ."

"*Indians behind us!*" a trooper shouted.

Then, as the Indians launched an attack from the rear as well as from the front, Reno ordered his men to mount their horses and ford the river.

Sutton dropped the carbine in his hand and made a successful grab for his Winchester before Reno had finished speaking. He booted the rifle, got into the saddle, and unholstered his .44 as Reno charged out of the timber astride his wide-eyed horse.

"Major!" Sutton shouted after him. "The wounded . . ."

Reno neither halted nor turned his head.

Around Sutton, men were mounting their horses and thundering after Reno, heading straight for the Indians in front of them and pursued by the contingent in their rear.

Sutton looked down at a trooper lying not far from Bloody Knife. The man, blood streaming from his throat, which had been torn open by a bullet, managed what Sutton thought might have been a smile. The man placed the barrel of his revolver against his right temple and pulled the trigger. As blood and bone flew through the air, an arrow struck the tree trunk next to Sutton.

He leaped into his saddle and flew out of the timber toward the Indians who were battling the troopers between the trees and the bluffs above the Little Big Horn. An Indian rode swiftly toward him, war club raised. The Sioux's war whoop died on his lips as Sutton fired, hitting the warrior in the chest.

The sound of small-arms fire and the vicious *ping, ping* of shots fired from carbines filled the air. So did smoke. Sutton rode on through the battling men on both sides of him, holding his fire, keenly aware of the fact that the troopers were not firing from the rear to cover their retreat.

A horse went down just ahead of Sutton. Its rider seemed to land feet first on the ground and was off and running as fast as he could go. An arrow pierced his body just below his left shoulder. He ran on for a few steps and then dropped to his knees. He began to crawl toward the river.

Sutton spurred his sorrel and headed for the trooper. But a warrior's bullet killed the man before Sutton could reach him. He rode on past the dead soldier, aware now of more men on foot running through the smoke. Behind him, the timber blazed. Ahead of him, horses were balking as they reached the edge of the bluff, refusing to jump from it into the river. Finally, after having been forced by their riders to jump, they went over the edge and, as Sutton reached the edge of the bluff, he saw that several of the riders had been unhorsed when they hit the water. They and their terrified mounts floundered about in the river.

He wheeled his horse and rode along the bluff away from the battle, looking for an easier place to enter the river. He never found it. A small band of Cheyenne were riding upriver toward him and he knew he had no choice. He turned his horse, spurred it savagely, and the sorrel leaped from the bluff.

Sutton remained aboard it when the horse hit the water because he had gripped it firmly with his legs, his boots out of the stirrups and pressed against the horse's belly. As the sorrel began to swim, Sutton clung to its neck, his face almost buried in the animal's mane in an attempt to present as small a target as possible to the Indians.

The Indians rode through the river on either side of the struggling troopers, picking them off one by one with both bullets and arrows as they would have done in a buffalo hunt.

Sutton kept his eyes on the bluff on the far side of the river. Directly in front of him, its sheer face rose, he estimated, a good eight feet into the air. But, he noticed, it sloped down to a mere three or four feet off to his left. He turned to the left, fighting his way through the river and through the screaming horses, some of them riderless, as he headed for the lower part of the bluff.

The Indians in the line on the left of the soldiers drove him back among the men and horses and, as he came closer to the far bank, the bluff seemed to touch the sky above it. Horses were trying to scale it, their riders clinging desperately, not to reins, but to their mounts' manes, to keep from falling.

The horses lunged, climbed up the bluff for a few feet, and then slid or fell back. One trooper slid over the rump of his horse and down into the river.

Sutton, as he moved up beside the floundering man, thrust a stirrup at him and, when the man had grabbed it, he rode on, pulling the man out of the water. He drew a deep breath as the man let go of his stirrup, spurred his horse again, and the sorrel threw itself at the bluff, feet scrambling, nostrils flaring, snorting loudly.

The sorrel slid back down the bluff and Sutton, looking behind him, saw part of the reason for his horse's failure to make it up the bluff. The man he had rescued from the river was holding tightly to the sorrel's tail with both hands.

"*Let go!*" Sutton yelled at him and, when the trooper didn't, Sutton holstered his .44 and pulled his rifle from the boot. Gripping it by the barrel, he swung it and its stock struck the man's shoulder. The instant the trooper let go of the sorrel's tail, Sutton again spurred the animal.

This time his effort to scale the bluff was thwarted by a trooper who was scrambling up it in front of him. The man lost his footing and fell backward, hitting the sorrel's head.

Sutton, his eyes stinging from gun smoke, tried again and this time he made it more than halfway up the bluff. Using his spurs, he urged the sorrel upward, swaying in the saddle as the horse lurched and fought desperately for its footing on the nearly perpendicular terrain beneath it. And then, after one final lunge, the sorrel was up and over the edge of the bluff.

Sutton halted the animal and quickly looked around him. Across the river, smoke rose from the burning timber. In the river, the bodies of dead troopers floated. The corpse of a horse, floating on its side, drifted downstream. Men were still fighting their way up the bluff, some mounted, others on foot. Sutton swung out of the saddle and knelt down to help a man on foot make it up over the edge of the bluff.

The man, he discovered, was Major Reno. "The Indians are riding up on the bluff from downstream, Major," he said.

Reno looked in the direction Sutton had pointed.

The Indians were riding almost leisurely, firing down as they rode at the soldiers below them who were emerging from the river, picking them off one by one.

Reno shouted an order to his bedraggled men on the bluff. They were to set up a perimeter on the downstream side of the bluff and hold off the approaching Indians. Sutton joined the hastily formed perimeter, lying flat on the ground and firing steadily, reloading, and firing again.

The Indians returned the fire for a few minutes but then

they turned and rode back along the bluff and down toward the river. The weary troopers lay sprawled on the ground, their clothes soaking wet, their eyes burning and half blinded by smoke and dirty sweat, their expressions listless.

"Major," said an officer as he and Sutton came up to Reno, "the men have been completely demoralized by the rout."

Reno seemed to spring to angry life. His eyes blazed as he stared stonily at the officer. "That was a cavalry charge, sir!"

Sutton couldn't help himself. The laugh that erupted from deep within him when he heard Reno's retort seemed to echo in the suddenly still air.

Reno ignored him and asked the officer, "Do you happen to know the whereabouts of my adjutant?"

"Lieutenant Hodgson's down at the bottom of the bluff, sir," the officer replied.

"Dead?" Reno asked dully.

"Yes, sir. He took a bullet in the leg and it went right through and killed his horse. One of the enlisted men gave him a hand out of the water but he was killed trying to climb up the bluff."

"How many men have we lost?" Reno asked.

"I don't quite know, sir," the officer answered. "I only just got up here myself."

"At least a third," Sutton said in answer to Reno's question.

"I started out," Reno said softly, "with one hundred and thirty-four officers and men. Sixteen scouts. A third, you say?"

"By my calculations," Sutton said.

Reno seemed to see Sutton for the first time. "Who might you be, sir?"

Sutton told him.

"You say you were scouting for Custer?"

"That's right. Just joined up, so to speak."

The officer said, "Major, we'd better make ourselves ready for the next onslaught."

"The next onslaught," Reno repeated wearily. "Of course, you're right." He looked around him. "Where is Custer?" he demanded of no one in particular.

Sutton couldn't answer him. Neither, apparently, could the officer because he remained silent.

"I thought he would be right behind us," Reno said somewhat plaintively. "I thought he said he would support us."

In the distance on top of the bluff, Indian sniper fire sounded. Many of the troopers, when they heard it, didn't stir from their positions on the ground.

The Indians below the bluff were fording the river, making their way back to its opposite bank, shouting and laughing as they went, and waving their bows and rifles in the air.

"Major," Sutton said, "look over there."

Reno turned around and his expression brightened. "Custer!"

"No, sir," Sutton corrected him. "That's Captain Benteen."

Reno began to run toward the advancing column of cavalry. "Benteen!" he cried. He waved his arms in the air as if he were afraid of not being seen by Benteen. "For God's sake, Benteen!" he yelled. "Halt your command and come and help me."

When Benteen rode up to Reno's men with Reno running along beside him, Sutton saw that he had brought not only reinforcements but also the pack train. A number of mules were making their way along the bluff, and strung out behind them in the distance were others.

Some of Reno's exhausted men roused themselves and began unpacking and distributing the ammunition the mules were carrying.

"Where is Custer?" Reno asked Benteen.

"I thought I'd find him here with you," Benteen responded, obviously surprised by the question. "He intended, I believe, to reinforce you."

"You can damn well see that he hasn't!" the exasperated Reno exclaimed.

"Odd," Benteen commented. "I received a message from him ordering me to bring the pack mules to the river. He said there was a big village and that I was to come on and join him quickly.

"I don't like this one bit," Benteen continued, frowning. "Trumpeter Martini, who brought me Custer's message, said he had looked back after setting out and had seen Indians firing at Custer's command from the brush. In fact, Martini himself was fired upon, he told me, and his horse was wounded.

"And then, after I had rounded up the pack mules and was on my way here, I saw Crazy Horse leading a band of warriors north. We expected them to attack us but they didn't. That scout of Custer's—what was his name?"

"Bloody Knife is dead," Reno said.

"No, I don't mean him. Or Bouyer. That other one. That half-breed. Johnny something."

"Johnny Loud Thunder?" Sutton asked Benteen, taking a step toward him.

"That's the one," Benteen said, nodding.

"What about him?" Sutton asked eagerly.

"He was riding with Crazy Horse."

"You're certain it was him, Captain?" Sutton asked.

"No mistake about it. It was him. Definitely."

"And you say Crazy Horse and his band were riding north?" Sutton asked.

Benteen nodded. "I wonder now if the reason they didn't attack us was because they had bigger game in mind. Namely, the highly renowned—largely as a result of his own self-promotion—Lieutenant Colonel George Armstrong Custer."

The bitterness in Benteen's voice did not escape Sutton. He turned his head and gazed north as Benteen asked Reno, "What do you think we should do now?"

"Dig in," was Reno's firm reply. He shouted orders and the troopers began to build breastworks of anything and everything they could lay their hands on—pieces of hardtack boxes, sacks of corn and oats, sides of bacon—and then to use their knives and tin cups to dig shallow trenches behind the breastworks.

"Listen!" Benteen said.

Sutton heard the faint sound of shooting coming from the north.

"Custer!" Reno declared. "He's giving it to those savages, I'll wager!"

The muted sound of distant firing continued without a break.

"I'll be leaving now," Sutton told Reno, who ignored him.

Benteen said, "Reno, we would do well to move out and help Custer."

Reno shook his head. "My men are exhausted. They need food and rest. The wounded must be cared for."

As Sutton swung into the saddle, Reno and Benteen continued to argue over the proper course of action under the circumstances.

"In the absence of specific orders," Benteen said, "soldiers should move toward the sound of firing."

Sutton didn't hear Reno's response. He rode down the bluff and the sound of firing grew louder as he rode closer to it. He began to feel excitement growing within him, an excitement born of the knowledge that he was riding toward his enemy, Johnny Loud Thunder.

And then, abruptly, the excitement he had been experiencing dissipated as an unwelcome thought crossed his mind. What if Johnny should be killed in the battle that was taking place in the north? The bitter thought that he might yet be cheated of the vengeance he had been so eagerly seeking for two long years soured Sutton's mood. He urged his sorrel into a gallop and minutes later entered Medicine Tail Coulee. When he emerged from it, the sound of gunfire in the distance was much louder than it had been back on the bluff.

Ahead of him, thick clouds of dust swirled in the air and through them rode hundreds of Indians. Sutton caught glimpses of blue-clad figures beyond the Indians and he knew he had come upon Custer's command although he could not see Custer himself. Indian Winchesters and cavalry Springfields were firing tirelessly.

Sutton halted his horse and squinted at the scene before him. As he watched it, Crazy Horse rode out of the billowing dust clouds. Riding with him were dozens of warriors. Just before the dust clouds swallowed them up again, Sutton recognized one of the riders.

Johnny Loud Thunder, his long black hair in braids and

naked to the waist, was wearing fringed buckskin leggings and moccasins.

Sutton fought the almost irresistible impulse to spur his sorrel and ride out after him. But he had a problem and he knew it. He put it to himself in the form of a question.

How can I kill Johnny and keep myself from getting killed by all those Indians in the process?

CHAPTER 11

His problem, Sutton realized, was more complicated than he had at first thought it was.

It would be—not easy, but entirely possible to ride toward Crazy Horse's band, who were attacking the Custer command and, once within range of Johnny, kill him with a carefully aimed rifle round.

But such a course of action was not acceptable to Sutton. Johnny, he told himself, has to know it's me gunning for him. Then he'll know why he has to die. Then I can kill him.

A rising wind was sending the dust clouds rolling away from the battlefield that Sutton was still watching and he was able to make out a band of Indians led by Chief Gall as they attacked the troopers from the south. The attack was a complete success, Sutton noted with deep regret. An entire company was wiped out within minutes.

Sutton suddenly saw Custer crest a low hill and wave a hand in which he held a pistol. Another company, evidently responding to an order Custer had given them, promptly moved over to the left flank of the command's position on the hilly ground—only to be as promptly annihilated.

Chief Gall aligned his warriors on the soldiers' left flank as Crazy Horse and his band made ready to assault their right flank.

Sutton was almost certain that Custer and his men, so vastly outnumbered as they were, were doomed. A sense of despair, of grim inevitability, swept over him. But then, as the warriors under Gall and Crazy Horse launched their separate attacks, Sutton spurred his sorrel and galloped toward the action.

"Johnny!" he shouted at the top of his voice as he neared the battlefield. *"Johnny Loud Thunder!"*

When Johnny looked back over his shoulder, peering through the thinning dust clouds, Sutton shouted a second time. "It's me, Johnny! *Luke Sutton!*"

Johnny turned away and Sutton thought he was going to continue riding forward but then he looked back once again and abruptly turned his horse.

Sutton reined in his sorrel and sat motionless in the saddle, waiting, hoping.

Johnny shouted something to a Sioux riding beside him and the Sioux shouted something in return. Johnny shouted again and waved his hand, which held a Henry rifle. Three Indians, all of them Cheyenne, wheeled their horses and rode behind Johnny as he galloped toward Sutton.

Sutton waited until they were halfway between the battlefield and his own position. Then he turned his horse and galloped away, glancing over his shoulder from time to time to make sure he was still being followed, careful not to get too far ahead of the Indians because he didn't want them to think they couldn't catch up with him. If they thought that, he reasoned, they might decide to give up the chase.

One Indian did give up the pursuit a few minutes later and went galloping back toward the now somewhat muted sounds of the battle he had left.

Three to one now, Sutton thought. Not real bad odds.

When he reached the entrance to Medicine Tail Coulee, he rode into it and then, after slowing his sorrel, he grabbed the rope hanging from his saddle horn and leaped to the ground. He ran in among the rocks lying at the base of the ravine and hunkered down behind them. Hastily, he formed a honda through which he slipped the free end of his rope.

As Johnny and his two companions rode past Sutton's position, Sutton leaped to his feet and, whirling the rope in a broad loop above his head, let it fly as if he were trying to head-catch a steer.

The rope circled Johnny's torso and his forward momentum pulled the rope taut, jerking him off his pony. As he fell, his Henry flew from his hand. Sutton raced over to where Johnny was trying to get to his feet and, as the two Cheyenne accompanying him turned and headed back toward him, Sutton unholstered his .44 and fired a quick succession of shots.

Both Indians fell from their ponies.

Sutton swiftly refilled the gun's empty chambers and then, turning the gun on Johnny, said, "Stay right there where you are."

As Johnny sat on the ground glaring up at him, Sutton backed toward the Indians he had brought down. When he reached the closer of the two, he nudged the man's body with his boot. Satisfied that the Cheyenne was dead, he moved on toward the second Indian.

He had almost reached the fallen warrior when the man suddenly sprang to his feet, blood draining from a shoulder wound, and pulled a knife from his belt. He lunged at Sutton, the knife's long blade glinting in the sunlight that was slanting into the ravine.

Sutton side-stepped but not quite fast enough. The blade of the Indian's knife bit into his left bicep. Ignoring the pain in his arm, Sutton fired at his attacker before the Cheyenne could make a second attempt to kill him. The Indian dropped his knife and fell to the ground where he lay writhing in the dust for several moments before he died.

"Get rid of that gun!"

Sutton spun around to find himself facing Johnny, who had gotten to his feet, pulled the rope from his body, and retrieved his dropped Henry. The rifle was aimed directly at Sutton's mid-section.

"Throw it over here!" Johnny ordered.

Sutton hesitated a moment, glanced at the rifle's muzzle, and then tossed his revolver toward Johnny. It landed at the man's moccasined feet.

"You're a long way from Texas, Sutton," Johnny said coldly.

"I am."

"I thought Foss had killed you that night."

"I guess he thought so too."

"I didn't shoot your brother," Johnny said, taking a step backward. "Hawkins did."

"Doesn't much matter to me which one of you four actually put the bullet in Dan's brain," Sutton said, his eyes on Johnny's face. "As far as I'm concerned, you're all guilty of murdering my brother."

"Judge Sutton," Johnny said, grinning.

Sutton said nothing as blood from his knife wound soaked his shirt sleeve.

"Have you been looking for the four of us all this time?" Johnny asked, and Sutton thought he detected an edge of fear in the breed's tone.

"I've already found Hawkins and Beaumont. Foss too, only he got away from me. But you won't get away from me, Johnny."

Johnny laughed then and Sutton noted that his laughter was far from joyous. There was in it, he thought, a note of near hysteria. Was it the result of the excitement of the battle he had just been in, Sutton wondered, or was it the offspring of fear?

Johnny said, "I've got a rifle. You're unarmed. And *I'm* not going to get away from *you?*" He laughed again, somewhat shrilly. "It's going to be the other way around, Sutton. You're not going to get away from me."

Sutton looked down at his .44 lying just in front of Johnny's feet and then up at the breed's face.

"When I've finished with you," Johnny continued, "I'm going back and help kill off Custer and his men."

"You were scouting for Custer so how come . . ."

Johnny shook his head. "I wasn't scouting for Custer. He only thought I was. I was spying on him. I came back here to my people and, when we heard he was coming down from the Yellowstone to wipe us out, I went and hired on as one of his scouts. I kept my people, the Cheyenne, and the Sioux informed of all his plans and moves."

"Spying's a dirty business," Sutton said bluntly.

"So's stealing land from Indians like Custer helped do in Dakota Territory. So's killing Indian women and children the way Custer's men did when they attacked Black Kettle's camp on the Washita River back in '68."

Sutton put the plan he had formed in his mind into action. He swayed. He let his knees buckle under him.

"Don't try anything!" Johnny shouted at him.

"I'm dizzy," Sutton said. "I'm losing a lot of blood and I . . ." He let himself slump to his knees, his head falling forward. He propped himself up with his hands, shaking his head from side to side.

And then, in one swift movement, his hands closed on the dust beneath them and he jerked upright, flinging the dust he had scooped up into Johnny's face. An instant later he sprang to his feet. He kicked the Henry from Johnny's right hand as the breed frantically rubbed at his blinded eyes.

Sutton bent down and picked up the Henry.

Johnny cursed him, rubbing his eyes with both hands.

Sutton's finger tightened on the trigger of the Henry. "It's time, Johnny," he said softly.

"No!" Johnny yelled. "*Don't!*" His hands came away from his face and stretched out toward Sutton. Blinking, he stumbled backward and fell over a rock lying at the base of the ravine. "I told you, Sutton! It was Hawkins killed your brother!"

"Get up!" Sutton said. "I want you on your feet. I want to see you fall when I fire. The way my brother fell. The way I did when your friend Foss shot me."

Sutton looked away from Johnny as the sound of hoofbeats resounded in the ravine. Their reverberations off the walls of the ravine confused him. He couldn't tell from which direction the sound was coming. By the time he realized that they were coming from the north, a band of Cheyenne astride their ponies came into view.

They saw Sutton at the instant he spotted them.

Sutton dived for cover in the rocks.

Johnny, blinking rapidly, yelled in Cheyenne from behind the rock his body was hugging for protection from Sutton.

Sutton fired the Henry at the Cheyenne. He hit none of them.

Johnny threw himself upon Sutton, knocking the rifle from his hands. Then he released Sutton, grabbed the rifle, and climbed out from behind the rocks to join the Cheyenne, who sat their horses, their Winchesters pointing at Sutton, who was slowly getting to his feet.

As one of the Cheyenne made ready to fire at Sutton, Johnny knocked the warrior's rifle to one side and the shot went wild. He shouted something in Cheyenne and was answered by the Indian who had tried to kill Sutton.

The ensuing conversation was brief. When it ended, Johnny turned to Sutton and said, "The battle back there at Greasy Grass River—what you white men call the Little Big Horn—it's all over. Custer's dead. They're all dead!"

Sutton had been certain that this was the way the battle would end. Still, he felt regret that it had happened as he had expected it to. He regretted too that Custer had made the decision to divide his forces the way he had.

He kept his eyes on Johnny's face, wondering why the breed had knocked the Cheyenne's rifle aside.

"I'm taking you back to our village," Johnny said, answering Sutton's unasked question. "When the women have finished with the soldiers' corpses, I'm going to give them a real live body to play with—yours, Sutton. Have you ever seen what our women can do to a white man in the way of torture?"

When Sutton didn't reply, Johnny said, "Well, you'll find out." He spoke to the Cheyenne in their language and then, turning back to Sutton, said, "They're on their way to wipe out the pony soldiers we've got under siege on the bluff south of here." He picked up Sutton's .44, stuck it in his belt, and then turned and walked over to where his pony stood.

The Cheyenne stared impassively at Sutton, their Winchesters aimed directly at him.

When Johnny rode back to them, he spoke to them again and then, as they rode away, he spoke to Sutton. "Start walking." He gestured with his Henry.

"My horse . . ."

"Start walking!"

Sutton turned and headed for the entrance to the ravine.

"Faster!" Johnny yelled at him. "Run!"

Sutton broke into a trot.

When he came out of the ravine, he trotted to his left, heading south.

"Sutton!"

Sutton halted but he didn't turn around. When Johnny told him to head instead for the battlefield where Custer had been fighting, he obediently changed direction and set out for it.

When he reached it, he halted again, staring out over the hilly ground and the carnage that littered it.

Behind him, Johnny let out a whoop of delight. "Some sight, isn't it, Sutton?"

Sutton stared at the grisly sight before him. Every soldier's corpse had been stripped naked and every one had been scalped and mutilated with the single exception of Custer's. The slashed bodies of the men of E Company lay in a line approximately ten feet from one another and each of their faces had been horribly mutilated.

"Our women sure had themselves a real picnic," Johnny declared gleefully.

Sutton stared at Custer's corpse. The body seemed to be reposing beneath the sky, which had been deserted by the sun. He thought he detected a faint smile on Custer's face.

He noted the bullet wounds in the right temples of two dead soldiers lying close to where he stood. So they saved their last round for themselves, he thought. He looked down at the dead horses, which had also been savagely mutilated.

"None of these pony soldiers will be able to attack our people in the next life now," Johnny declared. "Our women have seen to that. None of them will be able to walk or fire a gun again in that life. They sure won't be able to have children!" Johnny's laughter shrilled in the still clear air. "Except Custer," he added, his laughter dying. "Well, I'll fix that little matter myself."

Sutton heard Johnny leap to the ground and then he was backing around Sutton, his rifle trained on him as he pulled a scalping knife from his belt with his free hand.

"Follow me," he ordered Sutton, stepping around slashed and bloody corpses. "But not too close!"

Sutton moved out, following Johnny, who was backing away from him, weaving his way, as Johnny was doing, among the dead.

When Johnny reached the spot where Custer's clothed and unmutilated body was lying, he said, "You're going to do the scalping while I hold this Henry on you. You know how?"

When Sutton didn't answer, Johnny said, "You grab hold of the hair and then you make a slit on the forehead just below the hair and you run your knife all the way around the top of the head and then you yank hard on the hair to tear it loose."

"You're going to give me that knife?" Sutton asked in disbelief.

"I am. I'm also going to give you a bullet or two if you make any false move once you've got this knife of mine in your hand." Johnny tossed the knife to the ground. "Pick it up and get to work on the general."

Sutton bent down and picked up the knife. As he straightened, his eyes met Johnny's. Neither man spoke. Then Johnny gestured impatiently and Sutton knelt down beside Custer's body. He got a grip on Custer's thick yellow hair with his left hand and, shifting position, lowered the scalping knife.

"*Scalp him!*" Johnny shrieked.

Instead of doing so, Sutton deftly twisted his body and hurled the knife.

As its blade entered Johnny's body just above his navel, Sutton was up and moving quickly to the side.

Johnny's Henry, as Sutton had expected it would, fired as Johnny's finger convulsed on the trigger.

The shot missed Sutton, who then ran up to Johnny, who had dropped his Henry, and pulled the knife free.

Johnny, his knees buckling beneath him, stood grasping his mid-section and gagging.

Rage roared within Sutton. "Do you remember how you almost slit my brother's throat the night he was killed?"

The rage erupted within Sutton as an image of his younger brother's corpse burned in his mind. He plunged the knife into Johnny's chest, hearing it strike a rib before sliding on into the man's body in search of his heart.

Johnny's attempt at a scream emerged from his lips as a bloody gurgle.

Sutton withdrew the knife and this time used it to slit Johnny's throat.

Johnny, blood flowing from the wounds in his chest and mid-section and spurting from the severed artery in his throat, slumped to the ground.

Sutton, rage still roaring within him, reached down and seized Johnny's braids in his left hand. Blood from the wound in his arm dripped down onto Johnny's black hair.

But he stopped himself just as he was about to begin scalping Johnny. Enough, he told himself, his chest heaving, his breathing shallow. It's time to let go. I've been tied to this breed by a blood bond for too long. But now he's dead. I've killed him. I'm finally finished with Johnny Loud Thunder. Now it's the wolves' and buzzards' turn to deal with him.

Sutton ripped the sleeve from his uninjured arm and wrapped it around the knife wound in his left arm. After knotting the makeshift bandage in place, he took his .44 from Johnny's belt and holstered it, after which he began to pick his way around the dead troopers' bodies, leaving Johnny behind him on the eerily silent battlefield.

He made his way back through Medicine Tail Coulee, searching for his sorrel as he went. When he emerged from the ravine, he had not found the horse. Nor was it anywhere in sight in the river valley spread out before him.

He headed south, no longer thinking about Johnny Loud Thunder. Now his thoughts were once again focused on Adam Foss, the only one of the four men who had been involved in the murder of Dan Sutton to have escaped his vengeance.

But he'd find Foss, he promised himself. And when he did, Foss would die.

Sutton walked on, a grim expression on his face, as darkness began to gather about him.